THE *Gargoyle* FROM GENERAL MANAGEMENT

ISBN: 979-8-218-27522-8

Cover design and stepback art by: Kate Prior

1

In the Monster Resources Manual, it says every creature's needs for accommodations will be met by Evil Inc. Specifically, Section 13.4.2C, subsection RESPECT FOR MONSTERS RIGHTS AND ANTIDISCRIMINATION says, "The Company will respect the rights of all employed monsters, regardless of oaths, bloodlusts, undead dependents, or physiological strangeness."

I know because I wrote it. I put the form for accommodations and accommodated leave where anyone who needed it could access it, and easily fill it out.

But in order to fill out the form, the company has to recognize your status as a monster.

According to Section 13.4.2F, the Company will never use personal information for any means other than business and will keep it under strict confidentiality. Such information will never be disclosed without explicit personal consent.

After the manager who hired me as her replacement put in her two weeks, no one at the office ever learned what I was. And I have kept it that way.

I've been getting away with it by the skin of my teeth, working mostly remote—going into the office only when it's absolutely necessary to make an appearance, to hand out pamphlets to people bumping up against company policy and bare my teeth at anyone I've opened a file for recently. I don't like going in because it necessitates putting on my face—mascara, lipstick, the rest.

"Gwen, are you there?" a voice calls out of the shimmering mishmash of faces floating within the summoning circle laid out before me.

There's a company-wide séance, and our Chief Evil Overlord has remarked more than once at how proud he is that he doesn't have to cajole us to get people to be seen. There's at least ten other people who, like me, have erased that part of the summoning diagram to avoid having to be visually paying attention. A couple weak bastards still buckled at his remark.

I'm not good at hiding that I'm less than thrilled to be talking to people, and making it look like I'm paying attention is more work than actually listening is.

I don't need to participate in company retreat planning bingo or whatever they're talking about. There was an email about this, with an itinerary attached, but we have to go over it all to waste time, I guess.

"Yeah, here," I answer, not looking at the séance at all.

"I can't hear you. Can you hear me?"

Sighing, I pick up my lighter and flick it over one of the candles that had burned out. "Sorry, I was muted. I'm here, and I can hear you just fine."

The blood drains from my face when I look at the summoning circle again and realize everyone else has dropped off the call. It's just me and the Chief Evil Overlord.

I have to pretend like I've been paying attention, and not been clicking through different job postings for the last half hour. I thought applying to new jobs would be easier this time around. After all, I've been here long enough that I could apply for something with a more senior job title. I shouldn't have to go through all the same self-doubt as last time, thinking I don't have enough experience under my belt.

But as I'm scrolling through listings that demand master's degrees, twice the industry know-how, and the enthusiasm of a person a lot younger than me, all it's making me do is realize I'm not even great at this job.

I swallow and try not to telegraph all of that on my face. "How's it going, Soven?"

The faceless, cloak cowl looks back at me with what I can only imagine is disappointment that I was clearly not keeping up.

"I received your email about the retreat."

"Oh! Yeah. That. Um, I just think, do you really need me to be there? I mean, it's really just the Sales team presenting about last year's revenue and our new products. I don't really handle any of that," I say, my excuses feeling weaker with every word. "I was thinking, it'd be a great time to get through a lot of paperwork and reorganize my filing system, y'know, since everyone else would be gone, I'd have a full week without meetings."

Not things you say to your boss's boss, really. But I'm desperate.

I had originally planned to just take the time off—before it was made clear that everyone was expected to attend the retreat.

"Not to mention, then we'd save the money on my travel and hotel—"

"Gwen," he says, crackly with static through the séance.

I fall silent.

My teeth worry into my lower lip. It would be so easy to just fill out a form, and get the time off, no questions asked.

Except, there would be questions, and uncomfortable looks, and gossip to field when I got back.

"It would be more economical," Soven agrees, and my heartbeat ticks up in a rush of hope. He continues, "Unfortunately, I do need you there. Kathy and Ted will be in attendance, and as their MR caseworker, you are best equipped to handle them."

My never-ending source of paperwork—Kathy and Ted. Their file is about a mile thick. Unfortunately, their jobs involve quite a bit of working together, but they can't stand each other, and send in complaints over every little thing: Ted is mad Kathy misspelled his name several times on their latest email thread with a distributor, Kathy thinks Ted is deliberately undermining her contributions, Ted thinks Kathy interrupts only him during meetings on purpose, etc. The list goes on. There's really nothing too small for them.

"Their new supervisor will be at the retreat as well," Soven informs me. "I would like you fill him in on the best conflict prevention solutions or strategies . . ."

I frown as he rambles about whatever it is he thinks I do around here and wait for him to finish. "Did we hire someone on?"

"Oh, er, the other office did."

The other office is a much smaller location. It doesn't have enough employees to justify its own MR, HR, or IT departments, so they usually have to submit a ticket to our office to get those problems solved.

"Yes, given their particular circumstances, I thought it was time they had new leadership. I sought out an expert in the field."

Oh, sure, an expert. Someone who is actually going to manage Kathy and Ted and their problems instead of letting all the emails I CC them on pile up in their inbox.

He pauses, then adds with just a hint of excitement, "We snagged him from a much bigger company. You might have heard of him, Vladyr Grotesce."

"Oh. Wow," I reply, unable to fake my enthusiasm.

I wonder what kind of iron-fist type leadership guru Soven has in mind. Just one more thing I really can't stand, the kind of weirdo who posts long, practically nonsensical spiels on business forums about how keeping employees in office is best for morale, and then thinks a policy change tacked to the break room wall will do all the work.

Or possibly the worse option, someone who is actually hyper-competent and has centuries of experience under his belt, and a wall of awards and certificates to match. Just the thought of it makes me feel like I don't know enough to be here and that I'm going to have to bullshit about my own competency. Like his arrival means I've immediately forgotten how to do my job.

The call ends mercifully, with this week's prospects a little worse for wear. The last thing I want is to have to go through a thousand pages of complaint forms explaining Kathy and Ted's particular dynamic to a big deal manager who would be able to solve their problems in a snap and ask me why it took so long.

I really don't want to go to this retreat. I can already feel the ceaseless hunger starting to gnaw at my insides, insatiable and needy. If it's anything like the last time this cycle came around, I'm going to become a feral version of myself.

2

Don't book flights for work trips with anyone in your department. Have some work-life separation, for your own sanity.

I book my ticket on a red-eye flight a few precious hours before I have to "Meet and Mingle" with people I'm already cursed to spend eternity in daily conference call meetings with. I specifically booked a flight that wasn't listed on the shared spreadsheet, not caring that it was at an untenable hour of night. I don't care if I get an email from Accounting again about taking the same flights so that we can all carpool to the hotel from the airport; a girl has got to maintain her boundaries. The fact that you're staying at a gorgeous vista doesn't change the fact that you're going to be spending all of it with the same people whose meeting invites you've been avoiding.

I turn away from the ticket kiosk with the single-minded pursuit of getting to the terminal where my flight is, only to bump into my suitcase. It starts rolling down the incline to the airport security check without me.

My scramble to find any kind of traction in my slippers and chase my bag down is deeply inelegant, a flurry of sweatpants and unbrushed hair fighting against the unusually smooth tile.

"Come back, come back, come back," I hiss at my bag, fruitlessly. I didn't really expect my bag to listen, and it doesn't.

At least, not to me.

"You need to stop right there, miss," a fathomlessly deep voice commands, velvety low with a stern edge to it. My spine locks up.

I look up at the source of the voice, and the imposing figure whose shadow I've just slid into. He turns, the casual grace in the movement of his wings and tail becoming fluid yet formal.

Gargoyles are something of a rare sighting. It's a lot more common to find them at Fortune 666 companies in the Peak District, always wearing crisp suits and thick-chained watches.

This guy isn't any different, but when my eyes meet his, a deep molten amber, I feel the warmth in my cheeks burn through me like whiskey, spreading all the way down to my lower stomach. My posture changes like I desperately need to get a good grade in standing still, like that's a normal thing to want.

He turns around slowly to face me, and I'm a little taken aback at how my weird little presence could collide with someone as put together as him. In airports, at least, people this well-dressed slip past me as easily as oil and water.

My bag rolls until it collides with his leg, like a beanbag hitting a brick wall. I don't think he even notices, his eyes are so trained on me. The weight of his full attention is staggering. Maybe it's just that I haven't really been having face-to-face conversations with people much lately.

Ok, this is how I know my cycle is about to kick me in the face in the middle of this work trip. I'm never this easily interested in people right off the bat.

"Not you. You're perfect the way you are," he says, eyes never leaving mine. "It's just your bag that's disobedient."

"Disobedient," I repeat, perhaps giving away the fact that I clearly think he's gorgeous. His voice has a grip on me that is too easy to give into.

"Running off without you," he explains, offering me a little smile.

"Yeah, she's all hyped-up on sugar. It's all the plane snacks I put in her," I say. He's cute. He's very cute. Either this is a sign that I'm absolutely starved for connection, or he's downright charming. I honestly can't tell.

He chuckles, a sound that rumbles low through the portal and directly to my clit, bringing it out of hibernation. He smells good, inviting and warm, a little bit like a fireplace. I take an unnecessary step towards him, and I can feel between my thighs how instantly wet I am. My stomach feels warm as a tension-uncurling shiver moves through me.

Then something finally clicks. How my spine went rigid at his command.

Did I—no. That's not it. That wasn't what that interaction was. I did not just fucking cream my panties because some stranger was a little bit suave in front of me. Why wouldn't I just immediately do what he told my bag to do?

But he—

Pink creeps up in my cheeks.

I cover my mouth; even as he holds my eyes and his nostrils flare, and even though I don't know how keen a gargoyle's sense of smell is, I know *he knows*.

My cycle is starting, already. *Shit.*

I don't really know how to get out of this moment. I give him a brief little headshake, probably not doing a great job at concealing how little I want to be here. He nods and steps back a little, his large, bat-like wings flexing with the movement. They look soft, even with the stoney texture that sends cracks scattering through them like veins.

The space allows me to fully look him up and down, from the dark purplish-blue of his suit, the fact that he has a vest piece with a little gold chain leading into some hidden pocket, to the high arches of his hooves. My eyes linger low on him, on the shape of his long, thick, tapering tail that swishes gently behind him, moving gracefully with his wings.

He stoops a moment to find my bag's handle and rolls it back toward me. I take it, smile through a feeling that I imagine is what dying is like and turn in a different direction.

Well, there's the reason I don't leave the house, as if I needed reminding. I hate that it's only going to get worse throughout the work trip. I give myself a few moments standing outside the bathroom like I'm waiting to get in, willing amnesia into existence. When that doesn't work, I give myself a little shake and get on with my flight itinerary. It's fine. It has to be.

Drifting through the TSA line, I reassure myself that at least I'll never see him again. The world's too big to bump into the same person twice.

An airport worker opens the little crowd control dividers, releasing the stanchion belt and directing everyone stuck in my part of the line toward various luggage scans.

"Take out everything electronic, miss," a skeleton TSA agent tells me, just as I heft my carry-on bag into the bin.

I sigh, pull my work laptop out of the bag and lay it flat in the next bin with my suitcase, watching the one bin with my shoes disappear into the scanner. I always forget about that part. Before I worked for this company, I never had to travel so much.

The next TSA agent shuffles me through the scan and pat down, and when I come out, all ruffled, of the other end of this assembly line, there *he* is again.

The gargoyle guy is, of course, immaculately put together, tail flicking as he waits for his bag as well. He's got his eyes trained on the TSA agent going through his suitcase with unnecessary skepticism. It looks from here that someone's about to go through my bag as well.

Figures.

"All this hurry up and wait," I grumble out loud, sympathizing with him before I actually realize what I'm doing. I'm too used to just airing my thoughts to nothing and no one. I've really got to reign this in.

I attempt to exude an air of utter apathy when his eyes catch mine. It's what I do whenever I go to the office, mostly to try to cancel out the hope of being swallowed up by the floor. I've seen that happen to people at work, and there's nothing like a visual image for your social anxiety to latch onto.

He doesn't say anything at first, but there's a faint glimmer of recognition. I guess it was only a couple minutes ago that I nearly orgasmed in front of him, just from smelling him. I mean, he can't really know that happened, right? I wish I had the capacity to act like it didn't happen at all, instead of trying to still recover from it.

After a beat, the gargoyle offers in a low, almost conspiratorial voice, "Do you think we're being timed?"

There's really nothing to be said about airports that hasn't been said before. I can't think of anything normal to reply with, so I chirp, "It's training for a five-minute mile, that's why all the terminals are so far apart."

He doesn't laugh, which, ouch, but fair. I'm ready to just decide my ego shouldn't take any more hits from this stranger.

Mr. Overdressed-for-the-Airport offers me an arm to lean on as I hop around barefooted, trying to get my shoe on. Ok, that's sweet of him. A little old fashioned, maybe.

I lean on his arm and wrestle with my slipper to get it on over my now-sweaty bare foot, and he doesn't budge an inch the entire time. Maybe it's just the lingering shock of that weird little shared moment further back in the airport, but I'm a little impressed by his general sturdiness. Not that that's something to be impressed by—that's not a quality people say they're looking for, ever.

Maybe more is phasing me than just this gargoyle in his fucking three-piece suit who looks like he'd be easily cast to play a gentleman in a historical drama. Maybe it's the obvious intensity of the utterly different places we are at in our lives. Maybe it's seeing my greasy sweatshirt sleeve against the craftsmanship of his suit.

Generally, I don't care that some people wear their best business casual clothing to fly in; I'm firmly in the comfort category. I've got on the sweatshirt half of a velour track suit I've long lost the bottom half to, leggings, and slippers that have just enough of a firm bottom that I can pretend they're acceptable shoes.

Still, it does make me feel just a touch underdressed to be leaning on him.

"Where are you going that requires a suit this time of night?" I ask, because actually I've decided it is really weird for him to be dressed like this, now that I think about it. What are boundaries in the airport, anyway?

His attention dips down from whatever sign he was reading to me, and a wrinkle cracks his stony brow.

I make a self-aggrandizing sweep towards the rest of myself, fully leaning into his arm because he just does not budge. "This is me at my comfiest."

"Oh, that," he shrugs. He looks a little lost for words for a moment. "I . . . am also at my comfiest."

I blink, once, twice. I look him over again, to make sure his suit isn't just some really interesting footie pajamas I mistook for formal wear. It's not.

I'm sure that at this hour of sleep deprivation, I only barely conceal the sheer amount of "No, really?" that crosses my face. "I'm not judging."

"Just the smallest amount," he says, because I'm not fooling him.

"I mean, for a suit, it looks comfy," I try, and he rolls his eyes. There is a hint of a smile there. "If nothing else, it makes you memorable."

That gets him, and he looks away to hide the wider smile.

Just as I finish getting on my slippers, the bin full of my open suitcase and all the things that used to be neatly folded in it rolls down the ramp, along with the blue-latex gloved hands of the TSA agent probing through my belongings.

"Ma'am," the skeleton TSA agent calls, snatching my and the gargoyle gentleman's attentions to—oh for fuck's sake.

Is it regulation to hold it up so everyone can see exactly what I pleasure myself with? Was the luggage scan no doubt seen by a few more agents not enough? Because that one happens to be a silicone vibrator molded in the image of a chimera's cock—veins and webbing included.

Memorable is suddenly not such a great thing to be.

The TSA agent glances between me and my vibrator, gesturing me over.

I let go of the gargoyle's arm quickly, and step back. His eyes meet mine again for a fraction of a second before I'm ducking my head and sliding over to my bag, stuffing everything back inside.

"Believe it or not, there's actually more embarrassing things in my bag," I say, because ok, caught red-handed with a sex toy, but I'm not about to toss it out with my over-five-liquid-ounces of conditioner now. Then again, TSA doesn't harass vampires over their personal items when it's a suitcase full of blood pouches, do they?

Mr. Overdressed gives me a look, and at this point, I don't care. I can't. I'm beyond. I give him a deep stare of pure, unbothered apathy.

"You can't fly with these batteries," the TSA agent starts to explain to me, and I nod, watching her practiced hand open the end and pop them out. They land heavily in the trash.

Could have done all that with a little more subtlety, I think, trying not to grind my teeth.

When I get everything stowed away and my bag zipped up again, the gargoyle's gone. Not that I expected him to stick around or anything.

It's fine. I don't care. In a couple hours, I'll have forgotten he exists, and he'll have done the same for me.

I make it through the rest of the airport and waiting to board my flight without any more mishaps or making a fool of myself.

When I'm finally seated, I start pulling out everything in my bag that I need for my preflight ritual of Do Not Disturb. It's the main reason I started booking red-eyes I knew no one from work would be on. I would rather sit next to a two-headed baby where one head keeps waking up the other, than next to someone who is going to make me think about work for a four-hour flight. Two-headed baby doesn't care that I'm wrapped up in a lap blanket, an eye mask, a neck pillow, and noise canceling earbuds, creating my own sensory-deprivation experience with a true crime podcast to keep me company.

The last thing I want is to have to repeatedly unravel my cocoon for a coworker poking me awake with, "Gwen, what do you think about . . ." I'm not thinking about anything. If the plane crashes, it can do so without my awareness.

I play on my phone for a few minutes, before shooting an email to v.grotesce@evil.co.com, the address Soven gave me to forward Ted and Kathy's combined incidents records and get the new manager up to speed. On a whim, I search for Vladyr Grotesce online and of course a number of articles about some hotshot startup company came up first. Every few words I read into it I roll my eyes, and give up two paragraphs in before I give myself motion sickness. I know the type of guy he's going to be.

Hovering over my email, my company profile pops up: my name, a chart describing who I report to in the company, and a picture of me when I first started working there. It's such a stark contrast to see the younger, peppier, full of energy, smiling me with a face full of makeup and my hair curled. I try not to catch the reflection in my phone's screen—greasy blonde hair, my face sullen without blush to liven it up.

This Vladyr guy doesn't have a picture when I tap his company profile from the email address. His profile is significantly less filled in; he probably hasn't gotten around to it yet.

Then I put my phone into airplane mode, slip on my eye mask, and slip away from the world of the conscious, save for the occasional jostling of someone getting up from the middle seat next to me. I chose the window seat specifically so I don't have to get up for anything or anyone. I'm getting as much of the sleep I'm missing out on as I can.

My ears popping wakes me up when the plane finally lands. I'm slowly returning to the land of the living and undead, unwrapping myself from my sensory cocoon one item at a time, folding them carefully away into my once-meticulously packed carry-on.

I glance at my neighbor in the middle seat, and nearly break my neck on the double take.

Him. Again.

This is getting ridiculous.

He's also dozed off, his chin in his hand, propped up on the arm rest between seats. At least he's not awake to register my reaction.

I'm just about done squeezing the air out of my neck pillow until it's as good as vacuum sealed in its bag, by the time the gargoyle I can't seem to get rid of starts to stir. I pointedly look out the window and refuse to make eye contact, until I feel the row behind us start to shuffle out into the aisle to get off the plane.

"You're a sound sleeper," he remarks, several minutes into us both being awake. He's turning on his phone to an email notification noise, placidly opening it as people start getting antsy about exiting the plane.

"Yes, well . . ." I mumble, but stop myself before pointing out that I've embarrassed myself enough times in front of him already. A few times bumping into each other back in the terminal was enough, a whole four hours of sitting next to him probably would have chipped away at my remaining pride and revealed every overly personal detail about myself.

He doesn't let me trail off though. He raises a brow, and repeats, "Well?"

"Um. That's the advantage of traveling in your pj's," I shrug, and then bury my attention in my phone until we leave. I'm so done with this guy, handsome be-suited gargoyle or not. I'd like a little dignity to remain for tomorrow to pretend to enjoy my coworkers.

The one good thing about these corporate retreats to far away locales is that anyone you bump into, you're pretty much guaranteed to never see again.

3

I'm late for the first presentation of the company meetings, of course. Working from home, I can usually just open my laptop and attend meetings from my bed. No one ever notices I'm late or barely present. I always forget how much time it takes to do my makeup and hair and put on nice clothes with terrible, practically nonfunctional zippers. All so that I look like the put together, confident, competent person they remember interviewing, and not the greasy, pajamaed, boneless creature I revert to when I'm alone.

The meeting room is dim, half of the lights are off for the projector and our Chief Evil Overlord to give his welcome presentation. When I crack open the door, a number of heads turn to glance my way.

The conference room is laid out with rows of slim tables that sit two or three at each, arranged and angled, lecture hall style, to face the projector screen. Thankfully, there's a seat near the door still open that I can quickly slide into, even if it's next to one of my least favorite people.

"Gwen!" Deanna whisper-exclaims at me. She's everyone's favorite resident overbearing coworker who makes a competition out of being the nicest person in the office. Deanna grins at me and wiggles her eyebrows. She smells overwhelmingly like chipper positivity, sugar, and flowers. It's a little nauseating on an empty stomach.

"Did you lose weight? Sleeping enough? You look so . . ." Her brow furrows, and my expression pinches reflexively. Something more friendly, I think, trying to remember what that looks like.

People think they know what you look like, they really don't. They glance at your company ID and notice that your face is the same general shape, that your hair is the same color and about the same length. And for the most part, people have never questioned it when I look a little different every time they see me. People have never really noticed.

It's hard to explain how it happens. I can feel our chemistry as tangibly as I can smell someone's laundry soap or read their body language. The way I change to accommodate it is almost second nature, my features shifting ever so slightly, like pulling a smile into place or raising my eyebrows, until suddenly they're telling me how much I look like their ex-wife, utterly attuned to me. Or they're attuned to what they want, and I'm holding it in place for them.

Deanna shakes it off. She leans into my personal space and whispers, "What time did you get in last night?"

"Dark o'thirty," I shrug, attempting to match her smile through a yawn. It doesn't quite work, but she giggles anyway.

"You missed breakfast, but you can have one of the muffins I saved from the buffet," she tells me, and my grouchy, sleep-deprived ass wilts with gratitude.

She is genuinely nice. I don't hate her, or even really dislike her. I just know that she's the kind of person who drains me to be around.

"I owe you my life," I tell her, taking the banana walnut muffin and napkin combo.

"Don't worry, baby girl, I've got you," she smiles, clearly sated by my praise.

"Mm," I hum through a mouthful of muffin and a little bit of napkin. I don't care for pet names from coworkers, but it can't be avoided with her. I swallow and try to think of something that doesn't cross a weird line. "Thanks, darling."

She smiles, but I still inwardly cringe to hear myself say that.

Getting along with Deanna is simple enough, you just have to create opportunities for her to show how nice she is. If you try to be simply pleasant to her, you will end up trapped in an ever-escalating battle of wills to be the nicer person. "No, after you, I insist," ad nauseam.

Soven clears his, uh, nonexistent throat, and we stop our whispering and straighten up. I have my laptop with me to check emails and such, but there's never anywhere to plug it in so that it'll stay on for all six hours of meetings.

I keep my head down while I eat my muffin, trying to pay attention to Soven's presentation. The short nap I had between getting in from my flight and now wasn't enough to make up for the solid block of REM sleep I normally get, but it'll have to be enough. Maybe a few cups of coffee will keep me awake for the mind-numbing part of this trip.

After it's been long enough that hopefully most people have forgotten my awkward entrance, I wander to the little coffee bar set up in the back of the conference room, while Soven holds everyone's attention at the front. He absorbs the projector's light where he stands and almost looks flat against his "WELCOME TO THE 1043RD ANNUAL SALES MEETING" slide.

There's a lot of people I don't recognize, as I briefly scan the room. That makes sense, as Soven clicks to a slide about how all the new company growth has led them to hire a lot of new people. Then again, there's also just a lot of people I never really bothered to meet or get to know.

I empty a couple sugar packets into my coffee and stir a while, pretending to listen to Soven pontificating on our company values. I spot a little stack of notepads on the coffee bar, emblazoned with the hotel's logo. I grab a couple, since they each have about four sheets of paper. Some of my coworkers have notepads too, scribbling something every so often.

There's not a lot that means anything to me when it comes to sales numbers and bar graphs; I can't really tell what is and isn't confidential, and none of what anyone presents ever seems like something related to MR.

Maybe I shouldn't grab so many all at once, or someone will think I'm over eager to take notes. The thought nearly makes me snort out loud. As if. I'm going to do what I did the last three annual sales meetings: doodle.

The whole setup reminds me vaguely of being back in school; that while everyone else was semi-paying attention and even taking notes, my brain would shut off ten minutes into a lecture. By the end of class, the heel of my hand would be blue with the ink of my ballpoint pen and my notebook would be filled.

I'm more focused on stirring the sugar into my coffee than I am on the footsteps coming up behind me. The room is still dark for the projector, so I can't really say a shadow falls over me, but I feel it.

I note the three-finger shape of his big, stone-scaled hands with large dull claws on each tip, and the granite texture of the back of his hands. I know who it is before I even look up.

"Like a bad penny," a soft, deep voice rumbles, the hushed sound of it sends goosebumps up the back of my neck.

"Oh!" I gasp, and cover my mouth with my handful of notepads, shushing myself as a couple heads turn to glance back here and see what's the matter.

Deeply unfair, are the words that spring to mind.

Thankfully not my mouth, for once.

My eyes dart across the expanse of his chest, miles of it that there are, reluctant to find his face. But when I do, there's the face I've come to dread.

"More like a bad nickel."

He raises an eyebrow at me.

"I mean, I would like to get rid of you. Not in a threatening way, just," I smother that train of thought behind my fistful of notepads. "But you're a bit bigger than a penny."

Amusement flickers across his stony expression, before he returns in that low rumble of a voice, "And five times the bad luck."

He doesn't look any more bedraggled by the red-eye than he did at the airport. If anything, he's perhaps two percent more handsome than when I last saw him. I don't know why or how. Chiseled looks are an understatement. He has noble features, high, hollowed cheekbones, short hair that glistens like rutilated quartz. Ridges trace up his nose, over heavy granite brows to tall, curling horns.

It's the visual equivalent of stubbing your toe when you turn around.

He meets my gaze again and gives a little shake of his head with a smile that tells me he knows I'm ogling him.

And he's letting me.

Deeply, deeply unfair.

For a moment, I forget I was making myself coffee. I nod and just kind of stand there, clutching my half-made drink and several notepads as he moves closer to the table and plucks up a paper cup and starts to fill it with hot water, drowning a tea bag. Generally, I don't like to let people know when I find them attractive, because that opens the doors to flirting, and I cannot flirt to save my life. And I can't even imagine flirting with someone I've made a fool of myself in front of already.

Then again, maybe it's easier if we've already established that I'm a mess. I kinda doubt it though.

I watch him for a few moments, less stunned by the sudden abruptness of him appearing, yet again, and starting to sink into the why's and how's. I have no idea who he is, but I guess it's not completely out of the realm of possibility that he works at Evil Inc., and I've just never formally met him. He could even be from my local office, and it's just been long enough since I've gone in that I've never seen him before.

"Sugar? Milk? Organic orphan tears?" he murmurs, looking at me, and it takes a few seconds for me to realize he's eyeing my coffee for wherever my brain's stopped in this process. Oh.

"Milk."

I expect him to pass me one of the pitchers of varying percentages of dairy, but he takes my cup from me.

"How much?"

"Just. Um. Fill it the rest of the way, please."

I watch him make my coffee with an ease that suggests he maybe didn't see my vibrator being held overhead by the TSA agent. I'd like to crawl into that reality.

He hands the cup back to me and I'm not sure what to do with it. I'm sorry, why did he finish making my coffee? Is he fucking with me? Is this some weird powerplay because we keep bumping into each other? Or is he just being a gentleman and I'm too freaked out to see that?

"Thanks," I manage after a moment, failing to ask any of that. Maybe it doesn't need to be as drastic as I think. Maybe we can both just pretend none of last night happened, that we don't know each other at all. Because we don't, really, and it's unfair of him to hold any of what he witnessed of me at the airport against my character.

"Avid note taker?" he asks, attention falling on my handful of booklets and scooping a couple up. "I think I'll follow your example."

We're coming to the end of this interaction, I think. It doesn't matter that we bumped into each other in less than stellar circumstances, or that we work at the same company. I'm going to sit at my end of this meeting room, and let the memories be so smoothed over by meaningless statistics and pie charts, it'll be like none of it happened. By lunchtime it'll all be gone.

"Can you grab me one of those," he pauses, faltering for the word. After a moment he just opts for the word that seems a little more natural to the way his mouth moves, a mix of soft hisses against the audible grinding of teeth that makes a human in the last row of seats jump.

I don't speak it myself, but I recognize enough of it. Abyssal. Not an easy language on the enamels.

I pass him the cup of pens before he can confirm, taking one step away from the table as I do.

"Yes, pens," he looks at me with a piqued interest, reigning me back in.

Oh no. Oh no, no, no.

"Bilingual problems?" I ask in a faux friendly tone because this conversation has no reverse gear.

He nods a little, but now the gargoyle is looking at me with curiosity. "You speak Abyssal?"

"Oh, 'speak' is generous. Believe me, my dentist has discouraged me from trying. I already grind my teeth at night. But I know enough to get by," I ramble, the words pouring out without a thought.

He gives me that look most people do when I start oversharing, that hint of terror at being cornered with personal details in the most impersonal of settings.

I shrug, and add in the most emphatically casual tone, "I mean . . . I used to work in the Peak District."

It would sound smooth and less practiced in the mirror, maybe, if it had been the thing I said the first time.

Work is a generous way to describe it, but I've learned that people don't really want to know the details about how I interned and temped at a number of places, a lot of it unpaid. I didn't really do a whole lot there either, because most of the time my bosses forgot I existed. I spent more time getting people lunches than I did actually working.

His amber eyes light up, fully turning on me. "Small world."

"Very small."

Too small.

Another few moments pass, and I realize I've just been standing here even though I don't really need anything else.

I glance back to the front of the room, where Soven is clicking through some slides with graphs and struggling to use a laser pointer.

I give the gargoyle a little shrug and half-smile and flee back to my seat.

I hide my face in my laptop for a while, pretending to check my meetings calendar even though I have this week blocked off, and sending v.grotesce@evil.co.com a meeting invite for next week so we can further go over the whole Kathy vs. Ted thing. He still hasn't responded to my first email. I guess it's only been a couple hours. Not like he's going to need time to read over everything anyway, because he's not gonna read it at all, most likely.

When I've scraped back enough dignity to look up again, I find the gargoyle now has a spot in the front row, probably why I didn't notice him before. I wasn't exactly making the rounds with handshakes and clapping shoulders before the meeting started. I find myself watching the way he tucks his wings in close around the back of his chair, even though I keep purposefully looking away.

Man. My telehealth therapist is just going to love hearing about this.

4

This whole experience is one long social torture session, so, of course, there's a company-sponsored happy hour in the hotel bar.

And, of course, it's loud; it's a bar. Nobody's making bars where the music is at a reasonable volume, and they strictly adhere to the fire code for how many people can be in a building, and maybe the lighting isn't completely migraine worthy.

I was supposed to be watching Kathy and Ted, but I don't have the strength to seek them out, currently. I don't actually know what Ted looks like, and I think Kathy is avoiding me.

Right now, the plan is to have one drink, laugh at some jokes, set it down when it's empty, slip away like I'm headed to the bathroom, but make a turn at the last second for the elevators.

At least, that's the plan until the gargoyle from every time before fills the spot against the bar next to me. He's making eye contact at a level that suggests he expects conversation.

"Those meetings really took a lot out of me," I say, giving myself a little shake, and it's something. I can't keep remarking on the weather.

"Some of the slides are drier than others," he nods. "Did you take enough notes?"

"I filled two notepads, and I almost used up a whole pen," I tell him with just a hint of pride, because it is true. They're just a lot of doodles. But it's been a while since I worked with a ballpoint pen, and I'm rather pleased with how they came out. Normally I don't have the patience for stipple shading, but it works really well for the medium and, in five hours of presentations, I had the time.

I open my mouth to say something about all that, when our drinks are pushed at us, and the bartender is gone in a puff of smoke.

I pause, and push that thought away. I'm not going to tell him about myself. That way lays dragons. Or is how dragons get laid. I don't know. I don't want to mix work and my art.

"You must be more attentive than me; I only got through one," he returns, and it feels like a lie to just let him believe that. I try to tell myself I don't care because I don't know him all that well. But then again, I don't want anyone to think I'm super capable at my job and expect a lot out of me only to discover I'm actually just barely getting through it and faking that I know things.

Maybe it's fine. I probably won't interface with him much at work if I haven't talked to him up till this point. Still, probably better to not encourage that illusion too much.

Scooping my second drink up, I knock a sip back and fill my mouth with ice cubes.

I do know from doing it every day that the best way to avoid engaging with people is to be unengaging. I'm going to make myself boring. With any luck, he'll find an excuse to pause our conversation, and after about thirty seconds of sitting alone, I will be good to get back up to my room.

"I think I owe you a drink after this morning," he says in that lower-than-the-crust-of-the-earth voice. It cuts through the sound of the crowd and the music easily. I'm not really following his logic, but I agree. I'm owed many, many drinks, and a therapy bill.

"Does it count if it's on the company tab?" I return and feel very cool about myself for a second. Not so much when I have to repeat myself at not quite shouting volume just so he can hear me over everything.

He cracks a smile, and when I say cracks, for a moment I really thought it would break his stony features to physically move like that.

"It's up to you," he shrugs, unperturbed, though his eyes don't look entirely like he's networking.

I give him a once-over. There's some appreciative eyeing going on, I won't lie. I can't be blamed for what being in the middle of my cycle does to me.

"What are you drinking?" he asks, plucking up my glass from the bar and taking a sip for himself before I can answer. He signals to the bartender to send me another vodka tonic with extra lime.

It's a move that is so Peak District Suit that for a moment it's like I never left. Next, he's going to tell me I should invest my money in futures or whatever it is that these over-suave, financial analyst types say.

I hate that it kind of works for me. Even when I interned in the Peaks, I wouldn't let that kind of thing phase me.

My second drink arrives, and I take a sip from it. I chew my lip for a moment. No, it's a dick move, I decide. I'm also going to decide I don't like it.

"You seem like you want to share yourself with people. Maybe not every person you meet, but you're just brimming with things you want to share."

I try not to let my eyes roll out of my head. I can't tell if he's being sarcastic, or he genuinely thinks that.

"Second thought, I might just turn in early. I haven't recovered from that red-eye yet," I say, and kind of half-ass a fake yawn. I don't care if he actually thinks I'm sleepy. "Do you want the rest of this one too?"

He fits himself into the seat at the bar next to mine, in the corner by the wall. He turns the seat just enough to face more towards me, and lets his wings stretch out a little. "Not going to tough it out? People might not think you're a team player."

Good for him; he's stumbled into my two other least favorite things. Soldiering on when I feel like crap and team player rhetoric.

"Why does being a team player have to mean ignoring my discomfort? Doesn't seem like a good team to be on."

"It's playing the game," he shrugs, like it's that simple, and not the agony of trying to come up with any kind of conversation with coworkers. "Climbing the corporate ladder is a lot harder alone."

Of course, he sees it as vital to climbing up the ranks. That anyone who gets put in a position of higher management is there because they prioritize networking and the glad-handing circle-jerk.

It's kind of weird that a guy like him would be working at a small company like this one, now that I think about it. Gargoyles are kind of known for being ladder-climbers—top of the food chain kind of guys. There's a saying that if you need to find one, just go to the top floor of the tallest building around.

I can't imagine feeling that way. Not for a bunch of people who won't notice whether I stick around till the last round or not.

"Yeah, well. Game's rigged against us boring people."

"No one designed it to be fair."

My scoff is probably audible to half the bar. "Then someone should."

He crosses his arms and looks me up and down. For a moment, I think he's going to fight me on this. I feel the tension prickle on my skin.

Not throwing down with coworkers isn't usually on my list for how to behave at functions, but I may have to add it. After this one, at least.

I pick up the drink I was ready to let sit on the bar forever and knock back more than I should. Liquid courage.

"First of all," I punctuate with the glass clacking against the bar, "it's part of an unsustainable and expensive business culture. Burnout is real, and not taking care of people's needs means more turnover. Making things more fair with flexible scheduling and need-based accommodations helps you keep your best people."

He holds my stare through every word I throw at him. Is it getting hot in this room, or just my clothes?

"Second of all, it's more expensive to hire and train new people to standard than it is to keep your best people."

I wouldn't say those are actually two distinct points and not just a single thought I've split into two so I can sound like I've got more, but it's not like I had time to prepare. I think I might be melting under the intensity of his stare.

I think I'm killing it though. I've got him fooled. He's looking at me with a sort of fascination that I didn't expect. The room feels smaller and not so crowded, like I'm being drawn into him.

Because I'm winning.

"Third of all—" I cut myself off to roll the ever-dwindling ice cube around in my mouth, buying myself time as I try to think of a third good reason.

"You don't actually have to convince me, I was just projecting a little," he murmurs, as he sits back and runs a hand through his hair, loosening the top button on his shirt.

The way those small motions transform him from every other suit in the Peaks to someone a little more normal, it strikes me that you don't really find pockets of gargoyle populations here and there like you do with other cultures; every city seems to have a goblin market, an undead quarter, and an orcish grocery store; most cultures thrive from its community. After working in the Peak District, I never met a gargoyle that wasn't fiercely territorial and an overachiever to boot.

All of it combined with his little confession makes my brain short circuit. I almost don't believe that he just admitted as much.

"What?"

He shrugs, hiding just a hint of sheepishness behind his glass as he takes a sip. "I was convincing myself to talk to everyone in the room at least once, and then leave when no one was looking."

I'm so stunned by his comment, I can barely blink for a good, few moments. My posture shrinks a little. Maybe I was a little overzealous in sizing him up. I steal a glance at him again, and, somehow, now the bar feels a little less overwhelming in this corner.

"How come I haven't seen you at these before?" I ask, and realize I've reached the end of my third drink. I stir the ice around noisily until the cherry at the bottom is pushed to the top of the pile, and I can pluck it out and pop it in my mouth. When did I order something with a cherry in it?

I smile and feel the alcohol hitting my brain as my lips close around the cherry stem and my teeth separate it from the fruit. "I would have noticed you."

Oh, fuck. That comes off as too flirty, especially with the way I can't stop eyeing him. I clear my throat and try to regain some air of seriousness. "I mean. I've never met a gargoyle outside the Peak District before."

Foot, mouth, someone please help me. This is why I shouldn't drink with my coworkers.

He nods understandingly. He probably knows his presence is a little unusual. "The Peaks can be pretty cutthroat. I only worked there a century or so before I had to get out."

I believe him. Hostile takeover is an understatement for some of the acquisitions I've seen. I nod empathetically. "It's also just generally inaccessible. Especially for non-flyers."

"Exactly. If you don't fit into the very rigid work culture, you are ground into dust. It wasn't the way I wanted to live," he says, and it's a refreshing opinion to hear. I thought I'd never hear the end of how I wasn't climbing the corporate descent into hell from all my ex-coworkers.

I nearly tell him that, except my attention snags on the way he undoes the buttons on his cuffs, and, of course, Mr. Immaculate wears little gold and amber cufflinks to a casual hotel bar, paired with a thick-chained watch and class ring. I chew on my lower lip in an attempt to not be charmed by that.

It fails, because he begins rolling up the sleeves of his button-down shirt. When he sits back comfortably, the shirt strains across his chest, recapturing my undivided attention.

I'm weak. Oh, this is torture.

"This is my first one. I'm part of the company's new growth hires," he tells me, picking up his drink, about two fingers worth of a dark gold liquor. "But I've been at companies that partnered with Evil Inc. previously, before I decided to look for a broader managing position."

"No, don't tell me about it like you're about to hand me your business card," I moan before I can stop myself. It might be better if he did pass me his business card, so that I can remember I'm supposed to be networking or whatever, and not crawling into his lap so I can get two fingers of something else in me.

He doesn't crack a full smile, but I'm starting to recognize the hint of amusement the shadows carve into his face.

"I'm here to get to know people. Right now, my priority is to make sure everyone on my team feels recognized for the effort they make. I'm trying to come up with something better than these," he says with a chuckle, and shifting in his seat, he reaches into his vest pocket, and shows me a sticker sheet full of little gold stars.

"Oh, that's adorable," I laugh. "Forget whatever I was saying about retaining and appreciating long-term employees, gold stickers are where it's at."

He raises an eyebrow, but it looks like he's glad it amused me. "Not patronizing?"

"I don't know if you fully grasp how primal the need for a shiny, little sticker runs."

I wiggle my eyebrows, perhaps a little too drunkenly. Decorum is gone, I want a sticker, and I don't know how far I might be willing to go for one right now. Thankfully, I stop short of elaborating on that.

"Well. I usually try to include a note about the reason I want to recognize their work. I didn't think my last team cared about them at first, but they all started displaying their stickers where I could see them."

He pauses a moment, before sizing me up, taking a sip of his drink as he does. "If I were Soven, I'd give you a sticker for your retention proposal. It's a good idea, and, clearly, you've done the work to back it up."

That wasn't what I expected to hear, honestly.

My entire body heats up, and it isn't the alcohol. My insides are as gooey as molten chocolate.

I don't know if I wish he were my boss or . . . something else. It's hard to keep my thoughts from being horny about coworkers when I can feel my nipples harden at the thought of being awarded a sticker. I zone out a moment, wondering where he would put a gold star on me. Maybe somewhere sweet like my cheek. Or my collar. Or my hip.

No. The last thing I want is to get invested in the sort of guy who is only emotionally available for stock market shares and financial portfolios. Or maybe it's like the third thing I want, after a raise and one of those really big chocolate sculptures. I'm definitely not sober enough to put numbers on my priorities.

I stand with half a thought to step outside and fan myself off, and my heel snags on the damn barstool rung. Before I faceplant though, a clawed, tri-fingered hand catches me. His grip is stronger than mine, and it probably takes less than half of the effort to bring me to my feet and hold me steady.

It's a little too quick, being lifted from the ground, and I tilt bodily into his chest, my free hand thankfully catching me before I break my nose on his sternum. My fingers curl inelegantly around the seam of his breast pocket like it's a handle.

"Easy there," the gargoyle murmurs, too low to be anything but inviting, his tail flicking behind him. The rest of him is always so put together, so calm and collected in his perfectly pressed suits, but his tail gives off just a hint of his thoughts. I think I could watch it all day.

He raises an eyebrow—the ridge that is where eyebrows normally are but are stony scales on him.

He leans in close, and I inhale a little too sharply. The scent of him clouds my mind. I want to smooth my hands against his suit lapels, to feel the broadness of his shoulders. I want to so badly, I close my eyes and just let myself do it. I'm not going to think about any of the reasons I shouldn't.

Releasing my grip on his shirt and leaving a crater of wrinkles behind, my hand curls around his tie. I don't have enough boldness to reach for his horns, though I imagine that would be better leverage.

I can taste the scent of surprise on his breath at first, quickly overwhelmed by want, need, touch, crave. Feelings so primal they're easy to forget, but their subtle scent overpowers here.

His mouth is firm, not so soft and giving as other kisses I've had. My first instinct is to catch his lip between my teeth and drag them over it, sucking hard and then grazing my tongue over his teeth, the sharp and blunt edges a tease for what they might feel like across my skin.

His big hands span across my back, holding me gingerly. I feel the way he leans down to something more manageable for my height.

But I'm not here for a manageable kiss.

I reach up, the way I might normally grab a fistful of hair from the back of his head and find one of his horns to hold onto. His head pulls back just enough, opening his mouth more for mine. I pull myself closer, wrapping a leg around— either his hips or further up, I'm not totally sure. Somewhere in his middle.

He must not have been ready for me to launch myself into him, but his hands slide down to cup my ass, hoisting me off the ground. He keeps kissing me; every too-careful touch of his still pulling me further in. The notes of his emotions mix like a good cup of coffee, invoking floral, earthy, nutty scents that last only long enough to conjure half a memory—rainy days, foggy breaths against the windowpane, falling asleep in the middle of fresh laundry. A nostalgia for the home that exists only in memories, a nest. His teeth are sharp against my lips, his tongue sweeping over each brief nip, a salve of warmth for every piercing sensation.

I pull back for a breath, glancing around the bar. It's mostly emptied by now, and I don't see any coworkers. At least, none I recognize. My feet find the ground again with some uncertainty. I'm not sure if anyone saw us, but the worry still cools my libido a few degrees.

I look him up and down, really obviously, like I wasn't just kissing him for the past minute or so. I blink a little too slowly at him as I decide, hmm, maybe I do like him.

I'm genuinely considering inviting him back up to my hotel room for the night, and I think the same thought is crossing his mind. I can feel the way arousal moves through my body pushing the need to stretch, to straighten, to appeal to him. I don't hold back against the feeling, allowing my bones and muscles and skin to stretch into what feels right.

Then the bedroom look in his eyes falters. "You're not what you seem."

A needle of panic pricks the back of my neck.

"What do you mean?"

He tilts his head, and I watch his nostrils flare as he takes a deep inhale, and levels a curious look at me. "Not entirely . . . human."

5

I do not extract myself from this situation as gracefully as I would like to imagine. I flash a quick smile at him and immediately turn and bump into Deanna, spilling her drink onto my pants. Of course, then her need to be the nicest person in the room takes over; she drags me to the bathroom in a fuss and starts offering to grab me a pair of pants out of her suitcase.

"You know what, I'm just going to go back to my room to soak this, I'll just soak these and change into pajamas," I tell her, and after hours of yelling over music, my voice comes out much too loud, bouncing off the tiled bathroom walls.

Deanna looks at me with alarm and heartbreak. You'd think I had just told her that her baby isn't all that cute, actually. "You're not coming with us to the bar?"

I stare at her. "I went to the bar. We were just at the bar."

The thought of going back is out of the question. Even if I sit in a corner for the rest of the night and keep prompting Dan from Accounting to tell me about his pet untouchable slime so that no one else can get a word in edgewise, I don't have the stamina.

"No, no, sweetheart, not the hotel bar. There's another one down the street, it's open much later. We were all about to head over there," she coos.

Holy fuck. There's more? I didn't party this hard even in college. Why are my coworkers like this? A miserable feeling forebodes that I'm about to have to fend off the jeans she's foisting on me again.

"Oh. I don't think I could—"

"Come on," she says, and then wiggles her fingers like she's directing an orchestra. "Listen to the siren song of cheap cocktails."

I'm too stunned to cringe inwardly a little on her behalf.

I stare at her a beat too long and then clutch my head unconvincingly. "Ohhh. You know. I think I'm actually starting to feel kinda sick. Would you be a dear and see if the hotel store has any pain meds? I'll pay you back."

The opportunity for heroism in front of her overrides any further pestering about the second bar. She visibly brightens at the chance to channel her inner nurse. I can smell the enthusiasm and need on her. Terrifying.

"Oh, of course, baby girl," she coos, ushering me out of the bathroom with her.

"Thanks, uh, mama girl," I return, and I'm still too shaken to really care how awful that sounded coming out of my mouth.

We part at the end of the hallway, her jogging down to the hotel lobby store with a mission, and me trudging my way to the elevators.

I don't know how I'm going to survive the next few days of this trip trying to avoid that gargoyle. That interaction has left me feeling off balance in more ways than one. The way he was flirting with me, that kiss; it all has left my body thrumming with need for another taste.

But no one has ever noticed that I'm not human.

Sometimes people can tell. Usually, they can't. I don't tell people I'm a siren—almost never.

Too many people treat it like an invitation to cross boundaries they wouldn't normally. Telling people means getting harassed, and if I call them out for changing their behavior, it gets shrugged off because my existence is "asking for it." That's like assuming every undead you come across wants to eat your brains. They either expect I'm always down for a quickie, even if that's not our relationship, or that I should be interested in threesomes.

Every time it happens, I pull back a little more. The cocoon I've built in my apartment is woven a little tighter. Maybe there aren't more locks on the door, but opening it gets harder.

Being a siren isn't all bad. It means a lot of people want us for Monster Resources jobs. I can smell people's emotions on their breath, which I guess in theory would be useful, but it involves sitting a lot closer to people than is normal in the office, and I haven't really run into a situation where it gave me any more insight than someone's general outward attitude did.

But hiring managers think it's a good thing to have, and don't even care that I never finished my degree.

I ended up going into MR because it was a steadier option than anything I could do with my art. A consistent paycheck and health insurance for my soul. Like, literally. It's in my employment contract.

The hotel lobby seems empty until I round the corner of a large decorative pillar, and I'm halted by the sight of a harpy with her wings and a leg wrapped around an invisible man, the shape of him only visible by his clothes and askew glasses sitting on top of his head. Except, it looks like they were halfway through making him entirely undetectable.

A beat goes by, and when the harpy's face is a little less smushed by the kissing motions she's making, they notice me and startle.

"Oh," the two of them say, more or less at the same time.

I recognize the harpy from all my in-office meetings with her. Kathy, half of the bane of my existence at work.

I'm frozen beside them, unsure if I want to go back the way I came or continue past them like I saw nothing. The two don't exactly spring apart but they do detach themselves, re-buttoning their various undone buttons. I realize the invisible man's shirt has the Evil Inc. logo embroidered just above the pocket, so he must work with us.

"Uh, I'll, uh, circle back with you later, Kath," he says and hurries past me out into the hall.

I know that voice, that's the guy who's always calling me about Kathy's unnecessarily pedantic emails about less-than-prompt invoices.

"That was Ted?" The words just kind of haphazardly fall out as I glance back and forth between the harpy and the hallway his clothes have disappeared down.

"I've, uh," I pause and chew through "never seen him before," because that's obvious. "I've never met him in person before."

Kathy just kind of leans back against the hotel lobby wall and shrugs at me, not looking particularly cowed at being caught with her pants half off. She continues to fix her clothes. "Probably because he works at the other office."

"Oh." I nod. I don't know if I can process what I just saw. "I thought you two . . . well, I didn't think you'd . . ."

The words trail off with every thought I try to start, because I can't seem to figure out how to end any of them appropriately.

Kathy catches my eye, her usual glare much more striking from the side than it is from the front, like most birdish types. She knows I've handled most of her and Ted's complaints about each other, because she's the reason half of the time I go into the office for one-on-ones. Normally when she comes in with her coffee and catches sight of me, her feathers immediately bristle because she knows what's coming.

"What happens on work trips stays on work trips," she says simply, but the look in her eye suggests she doesn't want me bringing this up next time I have to schedule a meeting with her. "Seeing people from the other office doesn't happen often."

There's some smartass stuff I could say about maybe they should work together more often, but the alcohol is hitting my brain wherever it keeps my sense of balance. I cling to the wall for several long moments.

Honestly, I don't have the capacity to lecture her. I wish I could do that. It's been a while since I was with anyone, even a one-night stand.

It's also made more difficult because sirens need sex to survive. Well, that sounds kind of dramatic. I get all depressed and listless without it, the same as if I had a vitamin deficiency. The older I get, the harder it hits my body.

Sure, I could get it the traditional way, by seducing people and rawdogging their sexual chemistry like my ancestors did, before letting them get impaled on some rocks. But being around people drains me. Flirting with people on purpose makes me die a little inside. Seducing people is a lot of work when you're an introvert, and not actually a skill inherent to being a siren, despite the common misconception.

And even then, seducing comes with its own hurdles. Like, I get that people have to worry about getting pregnant and STIs and I want to appreciate that, but on the other hand, maybe a girl just wants to be fucked raw and whine, "Cum in me, Daddy," without explaining herself every damn time.

I sigh, and wave her off. "Yeah, ok. I didn't see anything."

Without even a "good-night," Kathy departs and leaves me sitting alone in the lobby, staring intensely at nothing in particular.

I lean against the wall and try not to let my thoughts seep with jealousy, because I'm not. Normally I wouldn't want anything like that, it's just that I'm in that part of the year I get supernaturally hot for anyone I have the barest amount of chemistry with.

I press my hands against my face. *That's probably why I launched myself at that gargoyle guy.*

My cycle is really trying to kill me. I don't remember it being this bad last time. I only felt a minimal need to hump my chair, not for an entire work conference. Yeah, there were some bones I wanted to jump, but it was never this desperate of an ache. I've never salivated over a granite carved jawline before, or wondered exactly how prehensile a tail was, and all the things we could do with just that.

It's then that I breathe in again; a whiff of a familiar scent, that fresh rain on pavement smell, makes my body nearly double over with that aching need again. The wave hits me so suddenly, it reminds me of the reason I left the bar in the first place, what I'm going to need to take care of.

A combination of things had made me flee—the question he posed, what are you, and the fact that the growl in his voice when he asked it soaked my panties thoroughly.

I needed to get out, I needed to tame the need clawing through my being.

There is a growing restlessness in my lower abdomen that will not leave me alone. This feeling has afflicted me before, but never had it felt like a fucking plague. It overwhelms my senses until I can't act like a normal person at this hotel.

The conference room we held our company meetings in is empty at this time of evening, and nearby thankfully. Slipping in quietly, I lean against the wall and unbutton my dress pants. Had it felt this pressing, this urgent, last time?

Last time, there wasn't a hot gargoyle every time I turned around. Last time I stayed home and ordered takeout and seduced whoever was delivering the food. There's a rush of excitement in me as I press back and slide my hands over my breasts. They are small, each barely a handful. My hands brush over my nipples, pinching and rolling them between my fingers as they pucker with pleasure.

When all this soft touching does nothing to truly satisfy me, I spread my legs and slide a hand down my stomach. I pop open the fly of my dress pants, while the other hand keeps preoccupied with my breasts, groping and flicking. I stroke slowly over myself, my hand brushing my lips, fingertips grazing more of my inner lips with each passing, doing little to relieve the need hollowing out my core. My body demands more, and I half wonder if it'll be enough to try to just satisfy myself. With a fingertip I find my clit and begin rubbing in circles. I close my eyes and imagine the gargoyle, tall and handsome, running his hands over me. I want to kiss, to mouth, to taste him, to touch and feel that hard muscle in my hands.

The conference room door creaks open, freezing me in the sliver of light.

I'm mentally composing my two-week's notice before I even see who it is, but when my eyes adjust to the harsh light, I find myself staring at a familiar tail, flicking behind well-polished shoes.

6

It's kind of inevitable that the gargoyle sees me, it seems like the sliver of light that catches me falls exactly on my hand down my fucking pants.

"Oh, hi again," I mumble at the floor tile, way too casually. I think about attempting to arrange myself into something less inappropriate, but my body is frozen. I mean, he must be able to sense whenever I'm in less than spectacular circumstances.

This is the night that will not end. I need to just climb into bed and reemerge again only for check-out.

"Are you alright?" the gargoyle says, surprise in his voice.

I'm just hanging out in an empty hotel conference room, masturbating, pondering my life choices, as you do.

"I, um, needed a moment alone," I tell him. It's as true as anything else I'm feeling.

My heart is hammering in my chest, but it also feels a little bit like it's doing that in my pants. The need to touch myself surges as I take a breath of him in. With how close he's standing to me, his scent engulfs my lungs like plunging into a pool.

I swallow, trying to steel myself.

I keep telling myself I don't care what this guy thinks of me. I don't even know who he is, really. But even if I can convince myself into utter apathy about him, my body doesn't get the memo.

I'm not going to touch myself in front of him. I have to draw the line somewhere.

He has yet to do the obvious thing, just backing away and closing the door, to pretend the split second he saw me didn't happen. I can't fathom why not.

Too many seconds roll by with us just staring at each other. I imagine loosely, it probably looks like I'm having an asthma attack or something, with how heavily I'm breathing.

No, who am I kidding, there's no way it isn't obvious what I was up to.

His eyes track over me, one hand down my pants and the other holding my tit. His nostrils flare infinitesimally.

"You asked at the bar, what I am," I say, my voice sounding just a little strangled and breathless as I try to hold back a moan. I try to think of a good way to say it, before deciding, fuck it, fuck me, fuck this whole trip. He's already seen my chimera cock vibrator, it's not like I had any dignity left with this guy.

"I'm a siren," I offer weakly. It's as much of an explanation of this as anything, the fact that my body is somehow more ready to go than it was before. "And I couldn't get time off during my feeding frenzy period . . ."

There's some noise outside in the hall, the sounds of people talking, and he moves closer, his figure in the doorway throwing a concealing shadow over me before the door closes and we're alone together.

I shuffle a little further inside to make way for his wingspan, and the movement jostles my hand in my pants and my fingers brush against my needy clit. I hiss at the contact, the sharp, all-too short note of pleasure and pain and relief.

I bite my lips and try not to rock my hips into my hand.

"I wasn't trying to, like, feed off your sexual aura before, when we kissed, I just," I fumble to say. I don't want him to think I was trying to use him before in any way.

There's so many different Sex Ed topics to cover, really only the most common types of beings are covered in public school. Humans have a menstrual period, harpies lay unfertilized eggs every so often, werewolves go into heat, orcs have the bloodfever, yadda yadda yadda. Sirens have a yearly cycle that causes us to prey on the sexual energy of random victims, whoever there's a spark of chemistry with to be had. Sometimes I think it's a little bit more like whatever vampires have going on, just not as often.

It's quiet, and I can only make out the outline of him in how dark this room is. I wonder faintly if gargoyles have better night vision and can see how hard I'm trying not to writhe against the wall. Maybe if I keep talking I won't feel the need to take a flying leap at him.

"A-and I didn't end up getting time off for it like I usually do, and I don't know how I'm going to get through this trip, but I just really needed to take care of this—"

"Is there anything I can do to help?"

An utterly baffling question to drop at a time like this, if you ask me. But the way he asks it, the genuine concern in his voice, I get that he doesn't mean it in a creepy way.

He's nice. And for some reason, that's weird. I can't help but be a little unsure of and mystified by the mere notion of being offered help when the corporate world is just a loop of shuffling your work off onto someone else.

"I can watch the door," he offers after a minute, and my body really, really wanted to interpret his offer in the most unprofessional way possible. "While you take care of things."

"Yes, that would be good. That would really help." I nod, even though I'm not actually all that sure how helpful that is, besides making him feel like he's helping me. But I'm so used to assigning busywork like that to Deanna that I just roll with it.

"Anytime," he says, and gives me a little half smile. I'm desperately thankful he doesn't press the issue.

He waits a moment, listening at the door, before opening it and dipping out. His tail brushes against my leg the slightest bit before he's on the other side, but that little graze lights my body up with need. I fall against the door as soon as he's gone, gritting my teeth as I resume my stroking with fingers now pruney from how wet I am.

I don't know how to process any of what just happened. Maybe I'm imagining it, but I think I can smell him through the door. I imagine him leaning on the other side of it, that I can feel his weight pressing against me through it.

The imagery makes me whimper aloud, and not a breath later, I hear him clear his throat on the other side of the not-very-sound-proofed door.

I don't have it in me to be mortified that I have an audience, rather emboldened by it. I want to know if he's listening as intently as I am.

My strokes become more vigorous, until I surprise myself with a burst of pleasure that makes me gasp aloud, and my thighs quiver, twitch, and shake. My hand is becoming slick, and I feel the heat in my body rising. With each rub, there's a short burst of unnerving pleasure and surprise that builds my need ever higher, but never high enough.

I wanted to feel someone else grip my thighs; to sink my hands into the gargoyle's body; to rake my hands over his chest; to mouth at his skin where I was lost for words from the way the shadows had cut across his form in the moonlight, showing the hard lines of his muscles and deepening each crevice; and to drag my teeth across his hipbones.

I feel my inner walls parting, anguish that there was nothing to fill the space as the feeling built. Spurred by horniness over self-preservation, I moan aloud, knowing he hears me. Whatever blood was left for my brain rushes south at the thought of what he might think, how it might make his body react.

I come too quickly, without enough build up to properly enjoy it, but it's enough for now. With a small cry, I arch off the wall, my knees nearly buckling out from under me. It feels hollow, unsatisfying, but it quiets the incessant need for a bit.

Maybe I should have asked him if I could just feed off his sexual magnetism in a work-friends-with-benefits-not-strictly-covered-by-our -health-insurance arrangement. That would have been so much more satisfying, but it would have crossed a line.

I open the door and slip out into the hallway, and immediately regret it.

"Shit. I think I'm dizzy," I mumble, and try to blow my hair out of my face to look at him. Earth-shattering orgasms aren't exactly a good thing when you still need to get back to your room.

He holds out a hand, and I awkwardly grab for it with the dry hand to steady myself. I don't usually need someone to keep me standing like a puppet, but climaxes have some pretty wobbly effects on siren bone structure.

It's hard not to remember the last time, only so many minutes ago, when he caught me at the bar, and how I'd just leaned into him bodily. I try to hold onto the fact of how very much I was not supposed to do that kind of thing, to avoid doing it again. I don't have the brain power to separate my horny, ungrounded in reality thoughts from, well, reality.

It doesn't help that I'm already missing the sensations that tasting him gave me.

"I think the others left for some kind of bar crawl," I ramble, trying to fill the gap of silence, to blot over the memory of this evening. "If, um, you were going to join them."

"Oh. No, that's not . . . not really my style," he responds, his voice soft against the vastness of the room.

"Well then. If you ever see Soven coming at you with green tea shots," I almost laugh. "Uh, go the other way."

His brow wrinkles. "What's a green tea shot?"

"Uh, matcha, peach schnapps, and something else. Something deadly, honestly."

He nods, and I hold myself on the wobbly precipice of not over-explaining that the only time I have gotten blackout drunk on one of these retreats is when I tried to keep up with an undead lich. Only one of you has a liver and consequences for it, but then again, only one of you is trying to make a good impression on your boss's boss's boss.

For a few moments, I just kind of stare at him, unable to think of what else to say. We don't exactly have anything in common.

I realize he's still holding my hand, probably for the better because I'm swaying on my feet. He has such a gentle hold. I guess it's hard to avoid crushing handshakes when you're literally stone. I feel like my hand is a bird perching on a skyscraper, which is not a sensation I'm familiar with. My chest is full of pigeons, cooing weird little confused noises.

His skin is somewhere between leathery and stoney, but the warmth of his palms softens his touch as he envelopes my hand and makes a shiver go up my spine. The feel of it makes me glance at his wings again and wonder what those feel like.

The metaphorical pigeons nesting in my chest are making more noises. The want to kiss him again comes back to me, a mental itch I can't just will away.

I look toward the hallway Kathy and Ted had disappeared down, feeling that pull of jealousy.

Kathy doesn't have the worst of ideas, though.

It's only the first day of this business trip, but maybe I missed the part where everyone introduced themselves to each other, and maybe I did it on purpose because nothing rots my soul like having to shake hands with people repeatedly, maintaining eye contact and a grin, while people rattle your arm, and hand you their business card, and begin to recite their resume at the same time, when all you wanted was to put names to faces.

It feels a little awkward to ask his name at this point. I had really hoped that at some point during our lunch or the hotel happy hour someone would have said his name, so I wouldn't have to ask.

"I didn't mean to offend you by asking earlier—" he starts to say.

"It's fine," I say quickly, swallowing.

He shakes his head, his twisted horns scraping the darkness of this hotel lobby. "It's not. Some things aren't work appropriate, and if I wouldn't ask it in an interview, I shouldn't ask it here. Some things are personal."

There's a strange, hard edge to his words when he says that. Personal. Though it pricks my curiosity, I can't help but agree, and for that reason I don't push. I'm grateful he understands.

"We haven't been 'work appropriate' since the airport," I sigh. "But thanks."

I manage to get out the half of the thought that is just gratitude, and less of the need to keep saying "It's fine."

He's holding my hand just loosely enough that I could pull out of his grasp at any moment, but strong enough to tether my swaying consciousness.

I find myself drifting closer, pulling in towards that anchor, and his tail gives a soft flick behind him, something amused in the motion. It makes me smile.

It's frighteningly close, and quiet. There's just the sound of our breathing, the moonlight glinting off his amber eyes as they sweep across me, dipping to my mouth.

Maybe this night isn't the trainwreck I think it is.

"I didn't get your name earlier," he says, the sound of his voice like a drop in a still lake, ripples of it reflecting off the darkened tile.

It would be so easy to just kiss him again. I don't have to take him to bed, maybe. It doesn't have to be preying on the sexual chemistry between us, feeding off of it the way my annual cycle compels me to.

Maybe it can just be nice.

"Gwen," I tell him, my voice nearly a whisper. "I'm from Monster Resources."

"Vladyr," he offers in return, something about the Abyssal depths of his voice goes straight to my clit. It does snag on my attention that he didn't say he was in finance or acquisitions. I don't think we even have those departments though.

"Hi Vlad," I echo, saying his name a little too much like I could stroke myself with it. It might be the vodka tonic that likes him. Weird how he's the second guy named Vladyr who works for the company—

I freeze, mid thought.

Time stops. Or maybe I just stare at him, eyes too wide for several moments.

I take my time, reevaluating my life, blinking at him. Vladyr Grotesce. The guy I have to work with on this trip. The guy who was most definitely going to make me feel useless at my job.

The same unmovable hunk of well-dressed marble that has already watched me make a fool of myself in every possible way.

7

I don't know how to describe what I saw this morning while heading down to breakfast, except to say I didn't know a disembodied voice and a black shadow of a cloak could wear swim shorts and flip-flops. I know that a few people wanted to take advantage of the hotel's pool before breakfast, but I was surprised to learn Soven was one of them.

Deanna sits next to me with her little bowl of yogurt, and every question she asks makes me want to sink into my chair and under the table a little more.

"Did you ever get some pain meds? Lily let me borrow some from her, but then I couldn't find you," she tells me, the most sorrowful expression I've ever seen on her, that she failed her mission.

"Um. I remembered I had a couple in my bag," I lie.

"Are you feeling well enough to be here? If you want to go lie down I'll let them know you're not feeling well."

"I'm just going to keep drinking water."

"That's what I should have done, honestly, after the second bar kicked us out after midnight. I swear, I'm still a little hungover. I got up late, at five, and went for a mile jog," she says. Just hearing her talk about jogging makes me tired.

As if I didn't already feel like death enough, my eyes find Vlad across the room. He navigates his way to an empty seat a couple tables away with a plate full of scrambled eggs and a glass of orange juice dwarfed by his large hands.

Vlad. Holy fuck.

I still have a few more days of meetings and being in the same room as him; what was I thinking, letting him guard the door while I rubbed one out?

What was I thinking before that when I kissed him at the bar?

Just looking at him right now makes me feel like I'm still interviewing for the job I've already had for years.

He must think I'm so unprofessional, getting drunk and sloppy and latching onto his face like some kind of primordial slime intent on devouring his soul. After I told him I'm a siren, I can only imagine that in his mind I've become some kind of twisted, preying creature intent on sucking his soul out through his dick.

Then again, how professional could he really have thought I was before, having seen my vibrator in the TSA line, I muse as my stomach roils with unease.

"Did the stain ever come out of those pants?" Deanna asks, bringing me out of my fugue state.

Vlad's eyes flick to mine, our gazes catching almost magnetically, and I think I've been stabbed in the chest. I drop my gaze to my shoes and seriously consider taking Deanna up on her offer to let me play sick for the day.

"They're still soaking in the sink," I lie again, because they're crumpled up on my hotel room's floor with the rest of my dignity. It wouldn't work. I can't play hooky every day on this trip.

When it comes time for presentations again, I sit on the far side of the room, putting as many chairs between me and Vlad as I can.

Our company's head of security—a giant eyeball creature I can't remember the name of—gives a brief talk about not letting anyone without a company badge into the office buildings to prevent more would-be saviors of the mortal world. I've been working from home enough that I didn't realize this was becoming more of a problem, but I also can't really give it much thought.

My attention has been creeping back to Vlad every ten minutes or so, just to check that he doesn't look like a storm cloud of invaded personal boundaries. He looks fine, I think. About as well-pressed and ironed as he usually does. He definitely uses those hotel ironing boards. I can't really tell though, because every time I glance back at him, he catches me looking and a shudder of awkwardness threatens to bury me.

I switch seats for this morning's presentations and sit next to Kathy for a change. I can't take much more of Deanna's endless positivity, how she's going to go for another run later, so she'll have energy for tonight. It's also more behind Vlad's chair, so he won't see me turning around to look at him so much.

Kathy acknowledges me with barely a grunt. She probably thinks I'm here to harangue her for MR reasons.

"How is it only ten a.m.? Kill me now," she grumbles, and it's a bit refreshing to find someone as miserable as I feel.

"No, me first. I've been to more of these than you," I return. Kathy conceals a chuckle in a sigh.

"Alright, no meetings for this morning," Lily announces, flouncing up to the front of the room, holding a little clipboard with the trip's itinerary on it. "Get ready, everyone, for a team building exercise!"

There goes any shred of hope I had for surviving the rest of this trip.

Kathy rolls her eyes and sighs. "See you in hell."

"I'll send the meeting invite."

We're hardly the only ones groaning, and it seems like this caught most people unawares.

Lily continues on, "Don't worry, they're not the usual icebreakers everyone's done a million times before. We put a lot of effort into finding some unique ways to learn more about your coworker's strengths and how to work more effectively together. Now, I want everyone . . ."

I squint at her a moment, not really listening. What exactly is her job title, again? Is she employed here or is she just always within haunting distance of Soven, little clipboard and three pens tucked into her little blonde bun?

I don't think I want to know, because honestly anyone who has mastered her level of organization kind of scares me. She sent me a spreadsheet once when I first started working here, and I immediately took that I knew how to use them off my resume.

The first icebreaker is attempting to get everyone in the room to count to thirty. I guess that means there's thirty people here, so you would think that it would be easy. But when two people jump to say a number at the same time, it all starts over again.

Unsurprisingly, this takes like a half hour to get through, and it's only stressful if you're paying attention. I don't think we actually make it through the whole count, because at some point Lily decides this is more time than she allotted for, and we need to move on.

"Ok, for the next exercise, we're going to try an arm puzzle!" Lily announces, and quickly starts dividing the room up. She clicks to a slide with directions and a picture showing a number of humans and monsters standing in a little circle, all holding hands with two random people across from them. I have a sinking feeling that I know this one.

"I don't have . . . arms . . ." Kathy starts to mutter to herself, because her "arms" are really more wings with clawed hands. It may look like she has elbows that bend in the same spot a human's would, but the bone structure inside is totally different.

Before I can suggest that this game is skippable, Kathy is, unfortunately, being pulled into another group. I blink and realize that everyone grouped up pretty quickly while I was standing around looking for a way out. If that's not a summary of my entire life, I don't know what is.

Lily's hand lands on my arm, and then there's her too-bright smile, guiding me over to the other side of the room.

There's little hope that this is going to be any better than trying to stay awake through another four hours of meetings.

"This group could use one more," she tells me, and when I look up, my face bursts into red at the sight of stone-carved wings.

8

There are a couple others in our group, but I direct my gaze to my shoes as I shuffle to stand in a little circle with them. I fold my arms and try not to look like I'm clutching myself, so that my facade of casualness won't unravel, even as I feel it slipping out from under my sweaty palms.

Even concentrating on the floor, I still feel the minute temperature difference from standing in his shadow, the way his wings hover inches from my skin. I breathe in his cologne, the subtle scents that make me think of hiking up a mountain, breath clouding in the cold air, and clinging to fir trees.

It's hard to resist glancing at him, and when I do, I catch him looking at me.

I turn my head away fast. He saw me looking at him.

And he was looking at me too.

After a few heart pounding moments, I sneak another glance, and he's looking away now too. I stare a few moments too long, too obviously, and he catches me again. This time I don't look away. I should. He smiles a little, and I return it.

"You'll have to introduce me, I haven't met enough of the other office," Vlad says to me, breaking our staring contest to glance at the others in our group.

"Oh. Um. That's Bill from Human Resources and Angelica from Legal, and, oh, Jessica All-Knowing-All-Judging," I turn my attention to the mostly shapeless concept who I had partly supervised during their internship last year; I'm a little surprised to see them here. "I didn't realize they hired you on permanently at the end of last summer!"

Jessica's shapeless presence crackles with electricity-like thrums. "Yeah, I'm on the Sales team now. I've been meaning to send you a thank you email for reworking my resume!"

"You don't need to thank me, it's all your hard work that impressed them."

"They wouldn't have known all the skills I picked up if my resume was still in shambles. I may be ageless, but I didn't have a lot of tangible, job-related experience when I applied online last year," Jessica crackles, explaining for the group's benefit. "You're so good at picking out skills people didn't even know they had."

"Oh, it's just adding in a bit of office jargon," I shrug. It's also a lot of bullshitting, but I think most people know that.

I try to focus on catching up with Jessica instead of the gargoyle looming over my shoulder, because if I look at him or breathe in more of his scent, I might combust in need of a follow-up for last night. And that really, really can't happen right now.

There isn't a lot of time before the instructions are given out for our next bonding exercise—reaching out and grabbing hands with anyone in the circle, letting our arms form a knot we have to untangle without letting go of each other.

I think I've had nightmares like this before.

When one of my hands finds Vlad's without really trying, I grit my teeth together and try not to think about it. I keep my grip somewhat loose and impersonal, but the clamminess probably gives me away.

Jessica hovers to the side, being shapeless and also armless.

"Come on, Jessica, you can take my hand," Bill waves his skeletal digits at the void.

"I really can't. Like, physically."

"Oh, be a team player, Jess," Angelica scoffs, her Can-I-Speak-to-a-Manager haircut swaying as she shakes her head disapprovingly.

A wave of defensiveness rises up in me, and I have to fight my knee-jerk reaction. Instead, I interject calmly, "Maybe Jess can direct us on how to untangle—"

"Oh, nonsense, we barely have enough for the game."

For what feels like an eternity, Bill and Angelica keep trying to get Jessica to participate, insisting that she is missing out on vital bonding experience, even though we're probably not all going to interact this much ever again. I think this exercise would have been smarter to do by department, learning how to solve corporate retreat-esque problems calmly with the people whose existence grinds away at your sense of self every day.

I realize that I'm standing closer to Vlad than anyone else. Bill and Angelica almost detach themselves to talk to Jessica.

Heat creeps up my skin, from my neck all down my back as I hold my breath and take in just how close we are.

His shoulder brushes mine, his wings are within grazing distance.

Now that I'm closer to him, I'm a bit warm under the collar. My thoughts stay on last night but take a different turn. What could have happened if I hadn't run from the bar, or if I had been unhinged enough to open the door and invite him back in; what it would be like to be intimately wrapped up in his wings while he rips my clothes off.

All last night I tossed and turned between dreams of what could have happened if it had gone further, and anxious nightmares of him hating me, being disgusted by me in person. I can only imagine everything I shared with him, any sense of understanding of who I am as a person, dashed out and reduced to a cliche, a siren trying to seduce someone minutes after meeting.

"I'm sorry about, um, last night," I mumble when it's clear our coworkers aren't really paying attention to the exercise, though one of my hands is clasped with Vlad's. I hope I don't have to clarify to him whether I'm apologizing for running out on him at the bar, or the drunken kiss, or masturbating in front of him.

Maybe all of it.

"No, don't be," he murmurs back, and for a moment I'm not sure I heard him right.

". . . Are you sure?" I whisper back, and then cringe at myself. Why would I not just be ok with the fact that he doesn't hate me for last night?

Probably because it means my libido will take that as free reign to daydream about kissing him again. I don't want him to be upset, but the possibility that he enjoyed it as much as I did seems dangerous.

There's something in the way his gaze lingers on the other side of the room by the door, the slow, fanged smile that graces his jaw that makes me realize I'm staring much too intently at him. I can't stop. His eyes fall on me, and it sends a wave of goosebumps up my skin.

"Yes, I'm sure," he nods, his brow lifting with just a hint of humor. "Let me know if you need me again."

Holy fuck, try to be a little less obviously horny for Mr. Broad Shoulders Department. Just because he's hot and surprisingly chill with my whole situation doesn't mean he's a good idea.

When the level of heat creeping up into my cheeks feels like it's going to combust, I promptly return to watching my shoes.

I literally just closed up a case at work where a human and an orc were being messily horny in the office, like no one else could see it. I mean, there's some pretty gnarly elevator footage, and no offense to Janice and Khent, but I wish I hadn't seen it. I don't have a mating bond to blame, though, just a mountain of paperwork that means I should know better than to mix business with pleasure.

Ten minutes later, I'm standing in the middle of a coworker knot. And it's significantly less fun than the kind of knot you might fantasize about being part of.

Bill and Angelica are supremely terrible at figuring out this puzzle. Jessica has disappeared to a conceptual restroom, and it seems like Vlad is doing most of the work in the group project.

"Alright, Bill and Gwen, move your hands over Angelica's head," he says, gesturing with his chin to our clasped hands.

I do as I'm told, and duck so that Bill can step over my now crossed arms, and twist so that Vlad's arm curls around me, as instructed. I clear my throat to disguise the noise I make when my back makes contact with his very solid arm.

This is torture.

I can't exactly strain away from Vlad like I'm repelled by his overly professional aura. I'm sure someone would notice. But it would be a lie to suggest I'm not enjoying the ways I'm too close to him—my thigh pressed wholly against Vlad's, or my back to his chest, or any of the other ways I can lean against him without anyone else's notice. I could be helping along with the puzzle more, sure. But his hand flexed and tightened around mine when I first did it.

I shouldn't be taking advantage of this moment, this puzzle. I'm just digging myself a deeper grave. But the way his tail flicks with a newfound energy, I can't resist it.

Every opportunity afterwards, I know I shouldn't, but I do it again.

At one point, Vlad pulls me in against him and effectively lifts me, decisively and easily, over the joined fists of Bill and Angelica and sets me, breathless, back on the ground.

Just like that, our little group is finished untangling ourselves.

"Vladyr! You should have asked her first," Angelica chides him, but my nethers are so very much about it. I would get back in line for that rollercoaster.

"It's fine. I don't know that I could have managed to step over you two in these heels," I manage to say instead of trying to climb him.

Angelica scoffs again, but wanders off with Bill, probably to ask Lily what exactly the rules are.

I have to seize on this moment alone with Vlad.

"Um, just in case it ever comes up. Don't tell anyone what I am," I say kind of weakly, snagging his attention.

I imagine he might think less of me for wanting to hide it. Not every monster has that available to them. But I can't trust everyone with that.

"A Monster Resources professional?" His brow creases, as he glances around us and murmurs, "Or a siren?"

I chew on my lip for a moment.

I don't know what he knows about my kind, but I know there's a lot to debunk when it comes to sirens. We're supposed to sing and seduce and lure men to their deaths.

Well, any gender will get the job done. We feed off of sexual chemistry. Personally, I've never killed anyone from feeding off them, just drained their aura enough to give them a hangover-like effect. And some of us, myself included, are pretty clearly tone-deaf. I've never convinced anyone to sleep with me by singing to them.

But the whole siren thing makes it hard to get close to people. Humans often think you're one of them at first, only to think you're a wolf in sheep's clothing when they learn what you are. Most monsters regard you as some kind of bottom feeder. Either people have specific notions of what I should act like, or they think I'm just sleeping with them to feed on them.

"People look at me differently. It's just . . ." I shrug and kind of half-heartedly try to explain it, when Lily starts calling loudly over everyone's chatter that we're done for today, and there's a half hour before dinner in the banquet hall. "I would just appreciate it if you kept it to yourself."

There's a question hidden in his furrowed brow, one that he's leaving up to me to answer.

Normally, I wouldn't. I really, really, really, hate every bullshit after-school special that implies that in order to authentically "be yourself," you need to share every little thing with people.

Like, what does that get you? Your identity stolen, usually.

But there's a gravity about Vlad, that I can't just break loose and leave it at that. I glance around, and thankfully we're pretty much alone.

Before I know it, I'm sheepishly shrugging and rambling, "It's more baggage than I want to bring to work. One moment people are normal around me, and then . . ."

I can't finish the thought. The fact that I have to split myself into the person I am every day and the part that has to bear the worst of everyone's assumptions, just to exist among other people, is already emotionally draining.

"Do you think you have something to be ashamed of?"

I'm quiet for a beat.

"No, it's just. If there was enough of me that people liked, maybe it wouldn't be so easily eclipsed by their pre-constructed notions."

"Like what?"

"Well, there's the usual bits, that I must be sex-obsessed and preying on people." I cross my arms around myself, trying to hold the feelings in while I let these thoughts see the light of day for once. "And sometimes for a bit of variety, there's the part where I only got this job because I'm a siren."

"Is that a thing?"

"I mean, you've witnessed firsthand what I'm like when I'm on my cycle," I shrug, making a self-deprecating expression. "It's not exactly a year-round thing."

"I meant the job part."

"Oh."

Several quiet moments go by. I contemplate telling him all of it, that I don't have a degree, that I dropped out of school, that this is the first and only white-collar job I've had that actually paid me, after all those internships commuting to the Peaks.

"Some people believe it helps with the job. There are more sirens in MR than any other kind of monster, statistically." I sigh weakly after a moment.

He nods, and I take that as enough to swiftly end that topic.

We're the last people to leave the room, but Vlad still traces one last, lingering touch low on my back. It's a move I'm familiar with, since it happened all the time in the Peaks, but it's the first time it's left me weak in the knees instead of rolling my eyes.

I follow without much thought into the hallway where everyone else is, floating in that feeling as he and everyone start to head back to their hotel rooms, daydreaming about wrinkling every inch of his perfect suit to such an extent that the dry cleaners would struggle to undo my damage.

It seems I'm not the only one. I can't say for sure that Kathy and Ted exchange heated eye contact, but Ted's clothes pass us by and Kathy shimmies in place like a bird repressing the need to begin her mating dance, ruffling her more colorful plumage in his general direction. Hell, I might have just looked like that a few moments ago.

She realizes I'm right next to her and whips her head around at me.

"I didn't see anything," I shrug, because her beak is very sharp. After a moment I add delicately, "What happens on work trips stays on work trips."

9

Once this whole trip is over, maybe there will be enough distance, or a therapist present, to help me sort everything into a neat little box. At least I've survived another day of presentations, and Vlad doesn't hate me. So he said. I don't know if I totally believe that, but, then again, considering how all the emotions I have about him right now are just too much to deal with here, I don't know that I could give him a confident answer about how I felt about him either. Weirdly fluttery? Mildly traumatized and aroused?

Until then, I just have to live without the feelings sorted. It's exhausting.

Of course, the moment I actually think I'm free to recover from that ice breaker, everyone's gathering in the hotel lobby to go out on another company sponsored bar crawl.

There's still two more days of this, and it already feels like I've been through a month of it. Back-to-back-to-back-to-back. There's been barely any breathing time, and now there's some kind of "fun city tour" event we're all supposed to attend.

Nope. I'm going to wander around the hotel looking to see if it has a spa or something. I need a little time not in a group environment.

I stop and lean against the wall to fix my shoe, and then pull out this trip's agenda, letting the flow of my coworkers pass me, chatting amongst each other. I pull away from the group as subtly as I can.

I'm waiting for the elevator when Vladyr spots me standing alone in the alcove.

He glances at me and then to the hotel lobby, where the rest of our company is already pouring out the doors and into a cab.

"You're not joining in?"

I toss my empty snack bar wrapper into the wrong bin by accident and end up fishing it out of the one that says REDUCE, REUSE, REANIMATE.

I shrug and chew the inside of my cheek to hold back the tirade about how I'm kind of at the end of my social stamina. An eight-hour day of mostly listening to my boss's bosses talk about things that I don't really understand is enough of being in a room with everyone. I don't think I could stand walking a few miles only to go into a smaller room where everyone is smooshed together at tiny, greasy tables just to drink together. There's a minibar in my room; I'll pass.

Besides, that ice breaker got me a little too warmed up to act normally around people.

"I'm gonna just hang out in my room," I admit a little too plainly, which, while shorter, probably sounds just as bad.

He raises an eyebrow at my bluntness, a hint of skepticism traced in his annoyingly well-carved features.

"Right. Not a team player," he says with a hint of good-natured ribbing. He glances at the lobby one more time, probably doing the mental math on that statement and how ready I'd been to climb him yesterday.

Of course, all the work I've been putting into cooling off and holding my need at bay disappears barely a few words into our conversation.

A flush of warmth overtakes my cheeks. My eyes rake over him without my permission. "Something like that."

The heat in my stare must be overwhelmingly evident, or he sees the way my features take the barest shifts to attune to him, because realization inches into his face.

"Oh. Oh."

I jam my finger into the elevator button again, and mutter with a little too much frustration, "Is it broken or something now?"

He glances around, cool as a cucumber. Or, let's be real, he's probably more like those prize-winning zucchinis.

I glance around and try not to utterly despair when the elevator doors open and there's a guy on a ladder in there, peeking out of the ceiling and clearly replacing a lightbulb.

I'm not falling apart at the seams yet, but I start to unravel, just a bit.

"Is it hotel lobbies that set this off?" Vlad asks. I think if I weren't horny specifically for the way he smiles, the note of amusement in his voice wouldn't have the reaction it has now.

"Yes, that's the one common thread," I sigh, pressing my face to the cold metal pane of the elevator doors after they shutter closed again. I'm dreading doing ten floors of stairs. I glance back to the conference room I'd used in a pinch last night, but there's some stragglers from the meeting still occupying it, chatting away like they have all the time in the world.

We pause in our little not-bantering, and I allow myself to look fully at him. He looks a little ragged himself. He still looks put together, of course, not a wrinkle on him. But there's a bit of wearing under his eyes from the long day, the top button on his shirt is undone.

I don't think I've ever salivated over a single undone button.

My attention holds on that little space of neck, collarbone, and the barest hint of chest that had been concealed until that moment. I feel like a period romance heroine swooning over well-formed calves, the way heat rises in my chest.

Distantly, I think about curling my fingers around the edges of his shirt in that space, and ripping it open, sending buttons flying everywhere. We'd never recover all of them.

No, no. Keep it professional.

He nods towards one of the hallways, a simple gesture that is too smooth for me to steel myself against when I spot the phone closet he's pointing out.

"Part two?" he murmurs.

My heart drops out of my chest and wedges into the spot between my legs.

This is the weirdest thing for work friends to do. Not that we're really friends. Or even work friends. I mean, I guess maybe we're friends? I like him well enough. He's nice, in a way that no one has been in a while.

The phone closet is small and a little dim, but there's a seat on one side and an old payphone on the wall, a dusty phonebook sitting on top of it.

He shuts the door behind me, I scramble to lock it before I can make a bad decision like grabbing his shirt collar and pulling him in with me. In my fervor, I slip an indelicate finger inside myself, stirring up the sensations that have been pooling down there.

It was still pleasure, but not as brazen and stark as when I stroked my clit last time, rather like a rumble from deep underground. It fills the space that is aching from emptiness. It is a soft, deeper feeling that brings pleasure gradually as my knuckles bump clumsily against my entrance.

I stroke, I thrust, and I grope, but it isn't working. This isn't doing nearly enough for me.

If this were any regular masturbation where I was just overstimulated and needed to cool off before I could finish, I would just tap out and try again later. But the need in my core is making my knees shake. The various feelings swirling in me are too much to just ignore for later.

I keep going, listening hard for any sign of Vlad, hoping to catch the sound of his breath, the shift of his shadow at the edge of the door, anything that would make the urgency in me burn readily like it was just a few moments ago.

Him being nearby isn't enough this time, and it feels like my release is ever further away, constantly slipping out of reach whenever I think I have it. My hands are tired and achy. As much as I want to stop and just rest, I think my body will feel worse if I do.

I let my head fall back against the wall and make a sound of frustration. I don't know what to do.

He answers the mere hint of my frustration, doesn't wait for me to ask. "Everything all right?"

I sigh and consider it.

On one hand . . . I could invite him in. Just the thought of him seeing me like this again sends a wave of want through me, a brief flare of need that I can't keep going alone.

On the other, avoiding literally masturbating in front of him might be the one scrap of privacy I have left.

Is that worth the gnawing need that will only grow if I can't finish it off now?

I free a hand from my endless stroking and twist the lock. The door slides open immediately just on its own weight, revealing how he takes up the entire frame.

"I need help, um," I stammer, a glimmer of reality catching my eyes. I don't have something planned to say to him, and yet the words, "please help me get off" aren't about to happen either.

Thankfully, he doesn't need the whole plea, just the one word.

Vladyr slips inside, in a movement that shows just how aware he is of the space he takes up. He tucks himself and his entire wingspan into the other side of the phone closet. Gratitude blooms in me that he doesn't make me struggle through asking coherently.

Just his gaze makes me unravel. It feels dirty and forbidden and everything I want.

I hold his stare a little too long while my cheeks heat, one degree at a time. It's not just some wild fantasy now, my coworker is taking up most of the square footage of an already rather small room.

I can see in his eyes the look of hesitation, looking for confirmation that I want his help.

"I don't know what's wrong with me," I tell him weakly, a confession that I never thought would escape me. I don't want to whimper in front of anyone like this, but I have no choice. "I can't finish."

"I'll take care of this," he says, voice soft and firm, and Evil Overlord help me, I believe him. I lean back against the wall and am all too willing to let him take over.

I don't think I'll ever recover from his stunningly low murmur snaking up my skin when he leans back against the other side of the phone closet. I could reach out and grab him if I wanted, and yet he's still too far away for my libido to handle.

I want him to touch me. I'm dying for it, but he holds back.

He takes his time, looking me up and down, leaving no molecule of me unscathed from his scorching gaze. The tight space we're in falls away, and I'm utterly exposed.

I'm pinned up against the wall merely by the weight of his eyes on me when he says, "Show me what you're working on."

Distantly, I think the number of embarrassments I've had in front of this gargoyle have trained the feeling out of me. A few days ago, I wouldn't have had the audacity or bravery to spread my legs further and run my fingers through my wet folds, but now I hold his stare as I do, and a new wave of need ignites in my core.

My hips twitch involuntarily, arching my back for balance against the wall, claiming another inch of the remaining space between us. I spread my legs a little wider, as far as the walls will let me, revealing my messy cunt.

I watch his nostrils flare and the way his chest and wings move, itching to spread to their full extent, when I drag my fingers through the slickest part, delicate lines clinging to my fingertips.

"Maybe there's another angle you could take this from," he says, his jaw tight around the words.

At first, I can't think what he means, before he offers his arm to me to lean on. I take it without another thought, his sleeve cool under my palm, my heart quickening. He arranges himself to kneel on one knee, letting me lean back against his thigh. I'm careful not to sit entirely against him, somehow the thought of getting any of my personal liquids on his suit is more mortifying than fingering myself in his lap.

"You know how to do this," he coaxes me, his voice a low rumble that nearly buckles my knees. His tail wraps firmly around my thigh, supporting my weight.

I don't know if it's the part where he believes in my competence, like it's an inherent, unquestionable thing, or the part where he's literally watching me finger myself, but it's what I needed.

I resume my work, but this time my own touch makes me twitch and hiss at the contact. Clearly, I'm starved for sexual chemistry if just being in a phone closet with him is enough to make me feel like this.

I delve my fingers back in, feeling how hot, slick, and unfathomably soft I am.

I add another finger inside myself, wondering how many fingers thick his cock would be. Touching him, breathing in his heady scent lights my mind alive with new, shameless curiosity. What it would feel like for Vlad to kiss my cunt, to lick me open, and fuck me with his tongue? Would his tongue have the same stony texture his arms, or more like his hands? My hips buck at the thought of his sturdy body bent over mine; a broad arm curled around my thigh as my knees rested over his broad shoulders.

"You're doing so good," he murmurs, something guttural in his chest. My eyes flicker open to sweep over him and catch a glimpse of the arousal making itself known in his pants. I have just enough self-control not to try to get a better look, and desperately wish I didn't.

With his face so close to mine, there's no mistaking the dark heat in his amber eyes. It spreads through my body like wildfire, and I tip my head back in a loud moan as my release takes me.

I spread my legs ever wider, fucking myself on the one hand as I rock my hips upward, and rubbing my clit hurriedly with the other. Different types of pleasure start building within me, each trying to speak louder than the other, calling and answering in a rhythm that runs faster and faster. I'm dirty and shameless, horrible and wonderful, damned and unbroken, and I love every bit of it.

I stumble to get up when the tides of my orgasm recede, peeling myself off of him. We don't say a word as we put ourselves back together into neater, less obviously entangled versions of ourselves.

I let my eyes meet his for the first time after we leave the phone closet to an empty hotel lobby.

He raises a brow. "Dinner?"

"Dinner."

10

Maybe I should have refused. I didn't realize, in my post-orgasm lack of brain, that accepting a dinner invite meant putting off my plans of taking my clothes off, laying in bed, watching TV, and wallowing in my usual anxious state.

Maybe I should let Vlad know that I'm the sort of person who needs to recharge her social battery with a true crime podcast for the next ten hours after talking to one person for more than ten minutes. But my tongue is pressed hard enough to the back of my teeth that I couldn't manage any kind of backing out.

We can at least get through dinner, and maybe we can figure out what exactly is going on between us, I reason to myself as I start to follow him to the hotel restaurant. I don't know about him, but I've never gotten off with my manager in a closet.

Just dinner.

And it's still a work trip, so therefore it's a business dinner, because it'll be reimbursed by the company. So, we're having dinner as coworkers, nothing else. I don't know why the idea of dinner is starting to freak me out. Everything untowardly horny between us has already happened, it's not like things can get any worse.

Maybe it's because it's a business dinner. He's already been intimately acquainted with the sound and sight of me orgasming in heat, but the part where I have to go and pretend to be good at my job when he knows I'm a wreck makes my jaw tense to new levels.

And maybe he isn't my boss, or department head, or anyone in my line of direct reports, but I kind of hate that he's seen all the worst sides of me first.

I hate always feeling like I'm lying to everyone about being competent at my job, but somehow someone seeing the truth firsthand is worse. I don't want to be seen for what I really am: a scattered mess of a person struggling with my body, because I didn't handle my PTO properly beforehand.

Things are quiet, even easy, as we arrive at the restaurant and are seated. We spend a few minutes not talking and just reading the menus.

It's a generic sort of place, fake plants, the utensils wrapped up in burgundy cloth napkins, that brick and faux industrial design that seems to be everywhere. There's a tealight candle in a volcanic salt vase, flickering between us as we're seated.

I hide my attention in my menu for as long as I can, because every time I look across the table, I'm desperately trying to merge the Peak District persona I expected with the person he's shown me he is and failing miserably.

Still, it's already nicer than going out with everyone else would have been. It might be the endorphins from earlier, or I might really like him. I don't know if there's a difference. A bit of tension that had been holding my shoulders up by my ears seeps away.

He already knows I'm a wreck. Maybe for once I don't have to pretend any differently.

The moment we give our menus to the waiter and have to look at each other, he folds his hands on the table and says, "I was actually hoping, earlier, to get a moment with you to discuss some things."

Terror, panic, fear. Tension returned.

"Something that wouldn't fit in an email?"

He shrugs, his smile easy. "Well, I have you here now."

After everything else, I don't know why that's what finally makes me blush. I bite the inside of my cheek to keep myself from telling him he can have me anywhere he likes. He's just helped me out of a couple rough spots, it's not like we have that kind of relationship. Do we?

"And besides. You've emailed me about them so much already."

Oh.

"Kathy and Ted," I realize, and let out a breath. "Those, uh, rascals."

"I wanted to discuss some of the mediation techniques you were currently implementing, and maybe take some of the burden with them off your shoulders," he says, and I don't know why it surprises me that he actually wants to do his job and not just leave me to handle it.

That gives me just a hint of ease, of warmth, before I realize—he doesn't know. I try not to immediately be weird about it, with what little control I have over that.

"Oh. Well. Um. My initial plan was really just to babysit Kathy and stare her down whenever she gets snide. That's not really an approved mediation technique or anything, but it's worked somewhat for me when we're in the office, so it's just kind of my off-the-cuff go-to. But, uh, hm," I ramble, and he has the gall to pull out a notepad.

While it's not an unusual part of my job that I have to inform someone's superiors that there's been some unprofessional intimacy, it's usually done through paperwork. I don't think I've had to do it face-to-face before.

"The other night, I was leaving the bar, and I ran into the pair of them, somewhat ruffled . . ."

"They've moved beyond passive aggressive fights, now?" he says, barely looking up from his notepad as he uncaps his pen and begins scribbling something out. He really thinks I'm about to tell him they just bitched about each other again. I guess he hasn't had reason to expect otherwise.

"In a dark corner," I clarify. "Sort of . . . entwined."

He slows down his scribble as realization dawns in his features. He glances up at me exactly once.

"Ah," he says, and then nothing else. He's quiet for several minutes. "Isn't that . . . against a rule, somewhere?"

I hold him in a stare. "Yeah, you'd think."

We're quiet after that, and I wonder if he's mentally tiptoeing around this as well. If it's against the rules for them to entwine at work, then shouldn't it be the same for us?

But we haven't broken any rules. At least, not yet. And this is a work trip. It's not strictly during work. We're not personally invested in each other the way Kathy and Ted are. I mean, I doubt most people have Kathy and Ted's specific relationship, but we're not like, involved with one another.

Not to mention, we haven't actually entwined anything, we've just been in the vicinity of each other's personal entwining.

But separately entwining nonetheless.

I shrug after too many beats go by. "I mean, they're not each other's direct reports. And they're not fighting as much when they're . . . well. I think they'll behave for this trip, at least. And when they stop behaving, maybe I'll just resort to blackmail."

It's not entirely serious, but it is a tempting thought. And maybe there's a chance they'll just behave better knowing that I know.

"Was there anything else you wanted to go over?" I ask, taking a sip from my drink and glancing at the notepad with only a few scribbles on it.

He sighs and drops his pen down on the paper. "Honestly, I thought that would take a lot longer. Considering the length of their file."

I snort. "This revelation is honestly making me rethink everything that's in there. It does shed some light on why nothing I did made them any less volatile."

"They didn't exactly cover arguing as foreplay in any management courses," he rolls his eyes, but there's a gentle smirk hiding in the corner of his mouth as he takes a sip of his drink. I watch his face, the way the tiny candle on the table throws shadows and light into the crevices of his features, carving into his pensive look.

"Honestly, it should be in there, because it's come up a number of times in my job," I return. "Nothing really prepares you for seeing your coworkers' asses out on security footage."

That gets a laugh out of him, and I savor the sound of it.

I catch a reflection of us in the glass partition between booths, and it's a moment before I realize it's us. There's something about the relaxed body language, his arm draped over the back of his chair, mixed with the semiprofessional attire we're both in. It reminds me of coming home from the office and kicking off my shoes to sprawl across the couch, stress melting away.

"So, this must be a fun introduction to the company," I offer, a weak attempt at conversation.

"It was something of a last-minute decision. I had it penciled in to take the time off. I've never been much for all the handshakes typically involved."

I remember the kind of crushing handshake battles that would happen between gargoyles when I was an intern. I can only imagine a younger version of him trying to avoid it.

"What made you change your mind?"

His answer is in his eyes before he even says anything. "I wanted to meet everyone I'd be working with closely, make some friends," he shrugs, and it's obviously a sidestep away from the emotions in his eyes. I can see I've struck something too painful for light conversation.

"I've been a boss for too long. Barking orders for people to get things done, burning through people's passion for their projects in the name of productivity," he continues, half talking with his hands and the delicate wine glass dwarfed by the size of them. "I wanted to be present, to meet people and get to know them genuinely."

"It's easy for companies to claim that everyone who works together is like family, to decide that if we say we're a close-knit group, that we'll be one," I offer, nodding along. I swallow, hoping to take this back to something a little easier for him to talk about. "But it's rare that it means anything."

His grip tightens on his wine glass just enough to send a hairline crack up its side, but not enough to shatter it. "Exactly."

I'm shocked silent by this as he puts the glass aside, barely acknowledging what happened.

After a moment, he continues, his voice low and gravelly with memory, "The last company I worked at was a startup I helped grow to be a decent competitor in its field. I was close with every member of our team. But when I needed to take time off for my health . . . it was easy to find someone who could do everything I did."

I watch the red wine seep out the crack, dripping down, silently bleeding into the tablecloth. After several heavy moments, I look up to Vlad's face. I want to reach across the table and reassure him he's not replaceable in the least. I don't know if it would mean enough, coming from me.

He doesn't need to continue for me to see how devastating that must have been when it happened. He gives his head a little shake and moves on. "It's rare to find a real friend."

I haven't had time to separate my first impression of Vlad from the marble man before me. But he is there, even if I couldn't see it at first past all the Peak-District-Suit-y-ness about him. He is so genuine in everything he's ever shown me. He didn't have to tell me about any of this, but he's been forthright from the moment we met.

I know that ache. That loneliness. To realize you don't even really have friends. I want to reach across the table to hold his hand, to tell him I'd be more than happy to have him as a real friend.

I start to make that movement but end up reaching for my napkin instead. I don't know that I'm capable of being one. Not under my layers upon layers of hiding.

"I'm sorry about the kiss," I blurt out. "It was unprofessional of me—"

"Gwen," he cuts me off, and I fall silent, my outpouring of worry stemmed by the look in his eyes. "You don't have to be sorry."

My teeth weld together against the onslaught of questions that creates. I want to ask him, "Why not? Doesn't it matter that a kiss can never just be seen as a kiss from a siren?"

But with those questions are more dangerous ones, growing out of an unearned, wildly misplaced hope and despair. I might as well demand to know, "Do you like me? Do you think I'm pretty? Or do you think I'm annoying and you're trying to politely brush me off? But just maybe, and hear me out, it sounds like you might kind of like me and my libido is all too ready to jump on that."

I need to stash my desperate need to be liked away. Holding Vlad's amber eyes, I nod, and bite down on my tongue to hold all those at bay.

He's right. It's nice to have someone here. And I've also really missed being able to just have a friend. I'm going to try to be that for him, and maybe it'll feel real.

Another glass of wine later, somehow we've gotten to a point where I'm rambling about a podcast I like and its anti-capitalist approaches to Monster Resources. "So, like, if you listen to a few episodes you might think the three hosts are, like, brothers, especially because of the name of the podcast. But if you've ever been to one of their live shows, you'd realize they're actually three heads of one hydra. Anyway, Justin's my favorite host-head because he has such great commentary on, like, consumerism being marketed to the public as how we should build our identities. You should really just give it a listen. You'll love it, I promise."

It doesn't really matter that I have yet to get anyone to listen to it with this tipsy pitch I've definitely given more than once before, I am just going to keep giving it.

"Anyway, one of their recent episodes gave me this idea to research unlimited PTO policies, and now I'm at the point where I kind of want to get Soven to implement one? Like, studies show people often end up taking about the same amount they normally do, though some people will take even less. That's something I need to read more on to see how to actually get people to feel like they're socially allowed to take time off. But the ability to choose improves morale regardless and ends up really useful for all of life's little accidents," I ramble, and I'm a little amazed I haven't lost him in this yet.

Vlad considers me thoughtfully, thumbing his chin like he personally carved that little divot in it. "And if they abuse it?"

"We can't continue to operate by expecting the worst of people. Assuming it'll be taken advantage of by a few people just makes us treat everyone worse. Taking care of everyone, including the slackers, is better for everyone overall," I say, though I probably fall into the latter category. Pantsless conference calls and playing Gourd Squash 2 during work and all.

"I can't wait for your presentation."

The enthusiasm I had for talking about my favorite podcasts and ideas dies out a little, and I try to keep myself from visibly wilting.

I don't have a presentation. Not that I couldn't whip one up and give a twenty-minute regurgitation of my favorite TEDtalks (Treachery, Excruciation, and Destruction), but there's no real place for it at this retreat. It's essentially the High-Fiving-About-Yearly-Statistics meeting, not the How-Can-We-Actually-Improve-Things meeting.

I also think that Vlad may also be overestimating my personal importance at the company.

The moment stretches, my silence aided by my repeated gnashing of ice cubes from my drink, whatever my dentist said about the health of my enamels be damned.

I try to shrug off the dip in my enthusiasm with a show of confidence I don't feel. "You should just give me my gold sticker now."

"You think you deserve a gold sticker," he says, clearly amused at my boldness.

"Yeah, I did my homework and everything."

He leans back and the motion makes me want to crawl across the table to straddle his lap. "I think I need to see a little more from you."

I bite my teeth on "I can show you my tits." That's not what he's asking for.

All the feelings I still have yet to neatly sort out in therapy roil in my stomach, sending heat up my spine. We just got back to a place of friendship, and now my body is ready to drive me into ruining it again. I have to remind myself that we haven't broken any rules yet, and we shouldn't.

After today's corporate shenanigans, his attention on me hits a nerve that feels like it's directly connected to my clit. I need it like I need my vibrator right now. What's worse, I think he knows the idea of the sticker strokes an itch in my psyche that hasn't been scratched in a long, long time.

"My impromptu song and dance doesn't do it for you?"

I recognize the look he has, it's the same as right before I kissed him in the bar. His amber eyes flicker in the candlelight, and darken as he takes me in.

The breath stalls in my chest as my heartbeat stutters. His eyes linger over me, in a way I'm not prepared for. "I'd like you to show me how far the need for a little, shiny sticker goes."

11

I've decided that I'm going to seduce Vlad.

Fuck it, sleep with a coworker. Maybe it doesn't matter. It's a work trip, it won't go on outside of that. Have some professional misconduct, as a treat.

It's not going to be in a specifically siren-y kind of way, like seducing him so I can get a good dose of vitamin jizz, but in a fun, I deserve to have a little bit of closeness with no strings attached. I would define everything else that's happened between us as pretty casual anyway.

If Kathy from Marketing can get her rocks off with someone from work, why can't I?

I'm tired of watching other people sleep with their coworkers without thinking of the consequences. I wish I could hold myself to a standard a little less than perfect without worrying that someone will think less of me for it.

Well, the decision comes less from taking a note from Kathy's book, and more from this morning's events.

I did not attend breakfast with the rest of the company like I had the other days—I intended to, but I saw Vlad in the lobby this morning and he fucking smiled at me. I immediately went back to my room and stripped down and used the entire battery on my vibrator in order to get through today. No, I'm not ok. I've never experienced a numbness and aching need like this at the same time.

It's not enough. I feel like every time I let my mind wander, I'm thinking about Vlad, being pressed up against him. I can't remember the last time I felt like this. I don't know how this is going to go away unless I sleep with him. I never would have been so turned on by a Peak District Suit like this, but he's charming in a way that's disarming.

Seducing him is how I'm going to get it out of my system. It'll be ok if it's just the one time. Work trips and all. Just one and done.

I don't really know how I'm going to go about it. I don't think I know how anyone actually does it, either.

I did spend a few minutes wondering if I should text my mom. She's a siren, she would know these things. But that might be considered actual torture.

So, I looked it up online. Did about ten minutes of reading. Set off with half a plan, because with more of one I might chicken out.

Pulling into the conference room, having entirely missed breakfast, I'm not confident I can pull off the whole seduction thing. I spent a lot of time leaning over the too-wide sink in my room's bathroom, attempting to draw symmetrical cat eyes, and they're still a little uneven.

"Baby girl, your highlighter is so good!" Deanna coos as I stop by the coffee table in the conference room, and it's sweet of her, if I were wearing highlighter. Guess my face is just always oily.

Confidence in this endeavor goes down a point.

"Uh—thanks, baby girl." I give her as big a smile as I can manage, because it's less emotional labor than letting her know that it wasn't the compliment she thought it was. I hate that "baby girl" is starting to enter my vocabulary from how much time I've spent around her. "Your hair looks great today."

She beams and turns around to her next victim at the decaf coffee station, and I take the opportunity to head to the other end of the conference room, escaping with my coffee and my life.

Even approaching him, now that I've made up my mind, I don't know how to behave. A sigh almost like a moan falls out of my mouth, and he turns to look at me.

I glance around and hope no one else heard that, not that there's anything I can do. We exchange quiet good mornings that feel achingly intimate, and yet not nearly enough. It's a bit weird, us playing around our coworkers like this.

"I saw you're on the schedule for presentations today," I tell him in half a whisper, because there had been an update this morning; an email sent out by Lily saying that there had been some changes made. I can't really squeeze my knees together standing without it being obvious, but behind the unimportant folder I picked up, I pinch my nipple in the hopes it will provide some small relief to the need between my legs.

"Miguel had to go home early, it sounds like his kid got sick," he nods, murmuring back in an undertone that makes me salivate.

Dark Lord, save me.

I bite hard on my lower lip to keep myself under control until I realize I need to reply. "And you already had one prepared?"

Because, of course he would. He has his life together; he's been in the corporate world a lot longer than I have.

"We collaborated on his presentation last week, but I added in a few more slides last night. Took a page out of your notes," he adds with a wink.

It's meant to be more casual banter than flirty, I think, but it still sends my heart skipping.

I chose a seat up front that's been vacant, a little off from the center. It makes a little sense that on the third day of hangovers, people's enthusiasm has died down and plenty are keeping their nose in their notes to hide their inattention.

"Well, I can't wait to see it. I bet you add all the best clip art to yours," I offer, then shake myself. Too office casual, I need flirtier banter. More seductive. I should have done more research.

"Well. I'll be up front. Give me something to take notes from," I wink back and immediately feel silly, but he smiles, and a herd of butterflies take off inside me. "Teach me something I don't know."

"Nonsense. I bet your presentation will blow us away," he says, as he watches me set my things up in the front row of tables of the conference room, my notepad and laptop claiming the centermost seat. I don't think I've ever sat in the front row before at one of these meetings. It's a lot easier to get through the day doodling and not paying attention from the back of the room.

"I'm not on the roster for today," I shrug, and it takes all of my willpower not to literally, actually, leap onto him like a pro rock-climber. "But it will."

There isn't any time for him to ask what I mean by that, as everyone starts taking their seats and someone turns the projector on.

Actually, sitting up front and focusing isn't as terrible as I thought it might be. Then again, my mind still isn't exactly on the topics at hand. Each presentation creeps by, and I'm doing the best I can to look normal while I keep my plan in mind.

Usually, I would be agonizing over whether people could tell I was wearing underwear in this skirt; now I've spent most of the meeting wondering if it's overly obvious I'm not.

This is kind of a leap, a bit of an assumption. Yeah, we've been flirting. I keep rationalizing it to myself. I don't think I'm actually off base here. Maybe if the kiss wasn't enough to demolish our friendship, maybe we could sleep together one time and be fine.

It's equal parts terrifying and thrilling and sets my heart racing to even sit on the precipice of my plan.

I've been sitting with my legs crossed tight almost all day, giving my knees a little extra squeeze together when it feels like I can't bear to watch Vlad from across the room. I don't know if it's because of my decision to go after what I want, or just the raw attraction he exudes, but the shift of his wings and massive shoulders together, how every half hour he rolls and stretches them, makes me have to fight to keep from chewing my pen open in my nerves.

His presentation is the last, and I wait until it seems he's halfway through his slides. I could watch him do this all day. The sound of his voice washes over me like a hot summer day, absorbing me in its hypnotic lull as he talks about numbers that don't really mean anything to me. He makes them sound compelling though.

The only thing that keeps me from forgetting my plan is my body thrumming with the need to climb him like a boulder.

I gather my skirt, my hands flat in my lap, inching up the fabric until it's just under unprofessionally short in my seat.

"The Dark Reign has been doing twenty percent better than projected for this quarter, but the question becomes, how can we make that growth sustainable for this company?" he says, and the way he makes eye contact with me and decisively clicks to the next slide makes me shiver.

I stifle a groan behind my hand and bite down on a knuckle. If he's going to keep talking about sustainability, I might climax in my seat.

His eyes linger over me, and I uncross my legs and cross them again—a brief flash of the fact I'm not wearing underwear.

His nostrils flare, and I have to press my knees together hard at the feeling of liquid heat that rolls through my body. I try not to just melt out of my seat onto the floor. Somehow, kneeling before him seems like an amazing and terrible idea right now.

My face feels like it's burning, even as I hold myself poised, waiting for it to end. My coworkers clap scatteredly as the "End" slide flicks by and the projector goes dark. All of it registers only distantly.

I get up just a little too early and leave the conference room first before Lily can even begin telling everyone what's next on the never-ending list of elbow-rubbing activities.

I make it to the elevator and press the button before I hear the conference room door open behind me.

It's him, just him, following me with heat in his eyes.

Oh no, baby girl. What have you done?

He follows me into the elevator with heated eyes, and I lean against the back wall, half hoping he'll pin me against it. His eyes are on my mouth, and I don't know that I have the patience for kissing, with everywhere else my body is begging to be touched, kissed, licked, everything.

"Hi, Vlad," I whisper, saying his name a little too much like I could stroke myself with it.

The distance between us starts to close as the elevator doors do. I clutch the railing behind me, nearly arching off the

wall in anticipation, if only to press into his touch that much
sooner.

"Wait, hold it open!"

My lust-addled brain falters for a moment, and I blink.
There's a lot I'd consider holding open in this particular
second but the moment I see someone's hand catch the
elevator doors, I just want to whine with frustration. The doors
trundle back open with resignation that feels all too
appropriate. I share a glance with Vlad, as he stands back to
let the guy on. I can see it in his expression as well, that
exasperation that we just can't get a moment alone.

Then to my horror, not just one person, but a whole bunch
hurry in, as if the elevator can't make more than one trip. Each
one of them asks for a different floor button to be pressed, of
course. Vlad and I are practically tucked into the back corner
with how many people have decided to gamble with the
elevator's load capacity today.

At least it's no one from our company who might have
wondered what we were doing so close to one another in the
elevator.

It's pretty packed, but not so much that I'm physically
touching anyone. There's maybe an inch or two of space
between everyone.

I startle a little at the touch I feel at my ankle, grazing
lightly over my skin. Glancing down, there's that flicker of

stone-gray scales weaving between my and Vlad's feet. I look at him, his wings pulled in close to give everyone more room, his shoulder barely brushing mine. He holds my gaze steadily and raises a brow a fraction of an inch.

His tail grazes higher up on my leg, and I realize he's asking me a question. My cheeks flush red.

I look around at the rest of the occupied elevator, but everyone is facing forward. No one is looking at us.

I don't know exactly what he's thinking, but I want whatever he'll do to me. I nod the barest amount, biting hard on my lower lip.

His tail curls around and snakes up my leg, digging into the soft parts of my thighs with a bruising grip. The tip of his tail skims up the sensitive skin of my vulva, tracing against the seam of my pantyhose as gently as a tongue might.

He gives an impatient flick against me, and I shrug the barest amount. Ok, I may not have been wearing underwear to the meeting, but I had to have something on, even if they're essentially see-through.

I bite back a moan as his tail hooks deftly against my pantyhose, carving open a seam for better access. He starts to drag his tail back and forth through my folds, slowly languishing, just a little bit deeper with each pass.

I nearly let out a groan when he finds my clit, needing to be touched.

He's teasing me, trying to pull any kind of sound out of me with his touches.

I have to be quiet, and that's not something I know for certain I can do. My fingers curl around the railing behind me, and I lean fully back against the wall, parting my thighs as much as I can in this tight space. He flicks across my clit again, and I nod again, trying to contain the shudder that moves through me.

How long can this elevator ride possibly be? I don't know if I can survive this. I'm biting my lip so hard I'm sure to be causing bruises.

The next floor comes a little before I do, and when the crowd empties out except for Vlad and me. I think maybe one of us should hit the emergency stop button, but he moves from my clit to my cunt, delving into me, curling deliciously in and out just as my release unfurls, clenching and spasming around the tip of his tail.

I let go of the support bar, and he catches me, holding me loosely against his hip. I'm too wobbly to really appreciate the closeness of our bodies for once. As the aftershocks of my orgasm recede, he traces a tender finger over my cheek.

"Good girl," he murmurs, and tastes the lingering wetness off the end of his tail. The low rumble of his words makes me warm at his approval.

I think I nod, but honestly there's a good chance I just stare, blissed out, at him, getting lost in the quartz flecks and inclusions in his eyes.

And then the elevator stops, the doors open, and he has to pull away. How can elevator rides be so short?

Someone a bit down the hall calls out, "Vladyr Grotesce! Just the gargoyle I was looking for."

The shout parts us. Displeasure creases his stony features with cracks as he turns to see who it is, and sighs.

Vlad steps out, giving me a little nod of goodbye, as I'm still panting and weak against the elevator wall. As the doors begin to close, I let my head fall back against the wall and whimper. So close, and yet so far.

12

All evening, I've been ruminating on the elevator.
Mentally, I have not left. Physically, I've finally let myself get
brought along on the company bar crawl, because when other
people got on the elevator, I didn't really know what else to do
with myself. I've been surviving the evening on soda and
water with lime wedges and humming along in agreement to
anything anyone around me says.

I wish I was only reminiscing on what it's like to be tail-
fucked, and I mostly am, but I'm also concerned. Somehow, a
quickie with Vlad was not enough to satisfy the absolutely
feral craving coursing through my loins.

He may need to come inside me so I can really feast off our sexual energy. I haven't done this enough to say that for certain, but I bet that will work.

It feels kind of icky to think of it that way, like I'm using him. But he knows what I am, and he followed me willingly into the elevator. I can't imagine he doesn't realize it kind of comes with the territory.

We're walking from one bar to the next after closing, never mind the aching feet from walking there in office-appropriate flats. Our group is passing back near the hotel again, and some of us are breaking off to head in for the night, while others are discussing where else is still open.

An icy breeze pushes past me as Soven whooshes up to the front to make an announcement before we lose half our people.

"Tomorrow we'll be starting with Khent's presentation with an update on our IT policies for next year, be there at nine. Until then, happy hour is in Iron Bar, tell them to put your drinks on the company tab."

People applaud and whoop, and I join in a little. It wasn't as bad as I thought it might be, but there are better ways to spend an evening.

My smile is pinched at best at this point, and I don't think I can tolerate another few hours of existing in a public space; I think I might be with the group heading in for the night. The only reason I kept with them for a few hours was the hope that Vlad might join us, since he was such a team player type and all. It wouldn't be the frenzied tearing his clothes off I'd been hoping for earlier, but it would have been nice to spend time with him.

The overheard mention of peach tea shots hurries me into the cab with a few other girls, some I still don't know the name of.

"That gargoyle from Business Development," one of them murmurs as the door slams behind me. "Is he married? He's cute."

There's just a few too many nods from the others in the cab. Kathy, thankfully, makes a derisive noise. "Ew, that's my boss."

"I don't think gargoyles marry, really," someone else says.

"Then he's single, right?" the first one continues.

My hand is like a claw as I fumble around for my seatbelt. I hum along, my teeth digging into my lower lip. It's like there's a spotlight on me, and one of them will notice it in a moment.

"Mm. I'm not hearing any of this," I add in a voice that is light, but just stiff enough to remind them I'm in MR, hypocritical of me or not.

Thankfully that's enough to stifle that line of conversation before it turns in a direction that is only marginally better.

"What's the juiciest thing that's ever happened at the office?" a vampire girl asks me.

Kathy makes a too-obvious death glare in my direction. Someone thinks a lot of herself. Still, I press my lips together and shake my head, to some groans.

"Well, I was on the floor below when Soven terminated Randall," Kathy offers after a moment, "The vortex nearly got me too!"

The ride is short, thankfully, and I manage to stay out of most of the conversation. We get out of the cab and separate, none of us really willing to hang out together.

The night sky looms overhead, little pinprick stars scattered through the greenish miasma. I don't know that I'll ever get used to it, seeing the cosmos this much closer. It's the little New Dark Reign things that really make you feel small and insignificant like this.

I feel a prickle on my skin as I notice a shape on the roofline that breaks the symmetry. A shiver crosses my shoulders.

Vlad.

My heart quickens, and I hang back from the rest of the group as they head inside, watching the silhouette of him stretching his wings wide against the moon.

I take the elevator to the top floor and find the stairs to the roof.

It looks mostly empty as I push through the door, walking the flat cement around the hotel's various vents, but I stop when I find him.

He's got one foot against the low stone barrier trimming the building's perimeter, his wings spread wide, the wind barely affecting them.

I'm struck, suddenly, by a wave of nostalgia for when I worked in the Peaks. It seemed like every office in the building had this kind of view. I don't see it much now, working at home with my screens. But it makes a different sort of sense now, knowing he is a gargoyle. I wonder what it means, what it feels like to need this kind of elevation as more than just a habitat.

And then he turns and looks at me.

I smile, unable to stop myself. "Hi, stranger."

"Hi, yourself."

He dips a hand into his jacket and pulls out the little pad of paper. By the way the corners have been curled up, I can tell he's been looking at the doodles.

"You left your notes behind from the last meeting."

Red rushes to my cheeks, to be caught not paying attention, to let someone see what I'm focusing on instead of what I'm supposed to be.

"Oh, my . . . really intensive and painstakingly detailed notes," I mumble, because it's pretty clear they're anything but that.

"I didn't know you were an artist."

"Artist, no. I'm more of a world-class daydreamer."

There's some kind of vent that has enough of a cubic shape that I can sit on it near him without getting too close to the edge. I can still see enough of the skyline, dark and swirling with mist.

"I noticed you're not on the presentation schedule for tomorrow."

"Oh. Um, yeah," I tuck some of my hair out of my face, glancing away. "You got me."

He's quiet for a long, long moment, and I can feel the way his assessment of me must be steadily lowering. I talked a big game about knowing anything about the field of Monster Resources, but it's all just things other people have said before me.

It's amazing that I've worked here this long without anyone discovering that I'm not actually good at my job and I don't have anything to contribute. I've just been getting along by the skin of my teeth and staying out of the spotlight. Maybe if no one notices that I'm not supposed to be here, they'll never realize that I'm not qualified to do anything that I do at my job.

"I don't really do anything important enough to warrant a spot in the schedule. I usually just send out a memo when there's a policy change."

I turn and look at him, and he clearly sees through me. I curl my arms around myself.

"And . . . there's really no point in me being here, at these big retreats. I don't know why they bother bringing me along," I finish weakly. I don't really know how to explain it.

He extends a clawed hand to me, and I stand, taking it. He leads me closer to the edge but encircles his arms around me. The wind up here is fiercer than on the ground, but with a big gargoyle protecting me, I'm not afraid of the height, or falling.

His voice is a low rumble in my ear that cuts through the wind and the noise of the city below.

"In the Peaks, it's easy to feel like a failure when you let society set the standards for you. It makes you forget what you wanted in the first place, when all you desire is to watch over what is yours."

I don't have the heart to look at him, to see the old scars in his features that I can hear in his voice. I just keep looking at the horizon.

"What is yours," I repeat, but the uncertainty I say it with makes it sound like a question.

He hums but doesn't answer. I'm not sure if he didn't hear me, or if he doesn't want to elaborate.

I don't press him for an answer. He's shared so much of himself with me, I almost feel it's greedy to want to know more. I'm starting to fully connect the things he's told me about himself over email and the person in front of me.

I turn in his grip, facing him. The soft, buttery smoothness of his suit under my hands contrasts with the breathing stone chest just beneath the fabric, and the muted heartbeat within.

Part of me aches to tell him that he knows what I am, he shouldn't be getting tangled up with me like this, revealing things that belong whispered in emails. But he knows so much of the rest of me, that I can't.

He draws the back of one granite claw along my cheek, before cupping my face and tilting my head up.

This kiss is different from our others, which were fueled by frenzied need. And while I feel it now, there is something decidedly less desperate about the ache in my core. Maybe the fluttering, cooing pigeons in my stomach know that there's something safe about Vlad. It doesn't have to be quick and artless, to get it done and get out before the wrong thing can be said.

I moan against his mouth, an indulgent sound. I want him to take his time with me. His hands slide down to cup my ass, lifting me up into his embrace. My hands find his shoulders, his horns, to pull myself further into his kiss.

During one of the breaths I come up for, I'm a little surprised to find that his leathery wings have curled around us, like a cocoon. I reach out and graze his wings, unable to restrain myself from the question of what they feel like any longer. His wings feel more like leather than stone, though each ridge of bone gradually feels cool and hard. His body shudders beneath mine, and I make a mental note of that for later.

He tastes like intangible things, and it's a shame scented candles can't invoke the thought of rainy mornings and crocuses in the early, dark spring, the air crackling with distant thunder. I would buy out the shelf of that candle.

I like him. I really, really like him. It feels kind of terrible that I'm going to feed on him for some vitamin jizz. (I forget what the scientific name for it is).

I stiffen at the thought and pull back from the kiss. Oh, fuck.

Here it is. The conversation. The part that means a hookup can't just be a hookup, because people think I'm using them as a meal.

I stare down Vlad, my lower teeth gnawing on the inside of my lip as I steel myself for what I'm about to say.

"When you fuck me," I start, because even if we weren't just talking about that, I have a feeling it's been on both our minds. Speaking clearly and firmly, holding his gaze, I say, "I am going to scream, 'Cum in me, now, please.' "

He doesn't blink, doesn't flinch.

I lift an eyebrow. "And I want you to actually cum in me. You can come in my mouth, or in my pussy, but not on me—"

His grip tightens around my wrist, cutting me off. I'd been looking at his face too much to realize the fucking brick in his pants now, the hard outline of his cock straining against the quality of his suit.

"If you keep saying that I'm going to teach you what you're asking for," he growls low in my ear.

Heat blooms across my skin at the thought. I lean in a little closer, holding his gaze. "When. You. Fuck. Me. I want you to leave me broken and crying for more."

13

My heart thuds in my chest as the door to Vlad's room closes behind us. His touch is impossibly gentle, every little graze building and adding to something in my chest that makes me want to cry out.

I'm burning to be touched; all I can think about is the need of every nerve in my skin. I hold still and try not to focus on how he removes my clothes so tenderly it hurts my chest.

"Wouldn't want them to wrinkle," he says of my blouse and skirt, folding them neatly to place aside.

"It wouldn't matter if they're wrinkled if you ripped them off me," I tease. I might have envisioned pulling the neckline of my blouse down, tearing a couple buttons off in the process, but his way is endearing. I definitely would have just kicked them off onto the floor.

He gives me a little chuckle in return. "Is that what you want?"

"I may budget for . . . shredding," I start to say, falling into a seat on the bed; I catch sight of him beginning to undress and my tongue doesn't know how to do anything speech related anymore.

I could watch Vladyr unbutton his suit all day. As impatient as I was to get down into his room with him, now that I'm here I'm happy to make time to just watch this. Lounging on his bed, I realize I've never really seen the appeal of a strip tease before, but maybe that's because they're usually missing the untouchable, unruffleable quality Vlad embodies so perfectly. I'm so caught up in the practiced motion of his hands I almost entirely miss the way he rolls his shoulders and wings, shrugging out of his shirt and suit jacket in one motion. I definitely don't catch whatever fabric mechanism is there to work with his wings so flawlessly.

I'm sure I'll satisfy my curiosity about how one tailors a suit to fit around a gargoyle's wings and tail when I watch him get dressed later. Right now, there are other things to satisfy.

My hands are twisting the sheets on his bed just so I can keep them to myself, and sort of tether my body in place. I feel a little like I'm underwater, or in a sauna, at my heat fully takes over, and I become immersed in it. It burns at my cheeks as the need to be touched, to be roughly handled and fucked into tomorrow until I can't hold myself up anymore eclipses every other sensation. I think if I just let myself exist in this moment unleashed, I'll just leap onto him and start grinding my hips against whatever is closest. So much is riding on the hotel's cheap thread count sheets.

Then his pants come undone, pushed down just far enough, and my eyes widen. Forget wings and tails, I want to know how his tailor works the fabric of time and space to make *that* monster hide.

I have girlbossed too close to the sun.

That's not going to fit in me. It can't. There's no way. Maybe I just thought I could flirt with the big gargoyle, and it wouldn't end with me being absolutely demolished, but I'm starting to think I was wrong.

The easy thing about long cocks is that there's only so deep they can go, considering my vaginal canal is probably at max five inches deep. But girth, you can quickly go wrong. One inch diameter? Meh. Two inches? Big girl games. Three? Getting concerned but it's still physically possible, I think. And we're at a wrong enough point that I'm seriously wondering, if I am going to have to dilate my cervix for this. I don't know how to do that.

Even from a distance of maybe like three feet away, the math isn't working for me. He's bigger than any of my toys and possibly my limits.

Rationally, I know that. Physically, my body has not gotten the memo. I've graduated from trying not to dry hump the bedding while I'm waiting to just not being obvious about it.

I've been staring too long, a sort of distress inching into my expression, no doubt. I look at Vladyr, trying not to convey alarm, exactly, but maybe concern.

Concern is definitely what he's looking back at me with.

I swallow. "Maybe we could start with . . . some fingering or something."

Then again, his hands are also massive. I did not think this through enough in terms of, like, sheer logistics.

But then something in his face shifts; that stoic look that I could easily mistake for being impassive has begun to make me feel warm and watched over. Like nothing bad could happen while I'm under the reach of his wings.

"Come here," he murmurs, pulling his belt out from his dress pants in a clean motion that sends a little zing of excitement through me.

I move to the edge of the bed, tucking my heels under me as I come to about eye level with the insane bulge in his boxer briefs and the thick trail of dense little curls that leads down his navel.

I watch him pull his cock out, unbelievably thick at the base, moving from the bluish hue of his stone to the leathery, purple, almost pinkish, still really thick tip. The patterning on his skin reminds me of pink malachite. There's a row of little bumps down the center of it, that snag on his thumb as he strokes himself for me; I can only imagine what they'll feel like coming in and out of me. I watch, greedily, as he gives his cock a few tugs, the way it just barely fits in his massive hand, the way the skin stretches and pulls with each stroke, the faint pulse of the veins that twine up the glorious length of it. Even hard, the sheer mass of it struggles against gravity.

The need pulsing between my thighs feels like it should be enough to make me climax, but the threshold for what will tip me over the edge has been supernaturally pushed back by my cycle. I try not to whine with just how needy and utterly empty my cunt feels right now, unabashedly rocking my hips against my ankles.

It's not until I open my mouth to speak, I realize I've been pressing my tongue hard against the back of my teeth this entire time. I swallow and offer a quiet, "May I?"

I don't know why I feel like I need to ask permission to touch him, just that he is always so perfectly pressed in his suits, not a line or fold or wrinkle out of place. Seeing him with his shirt unbuttoned, parted like curtains to reveal the dark wisps of marbling down his stone abdomen, makes me feel reverent.

He traces a finger under my jaw, tipping my chin upward to look him in the face. At this angle, I'm a little surprised I can make eye contact still, with his chest almost eclipsing my view.

There's a quiet vulnerability in his eyes, and I remember, just for a second, that time I bumped into him at the airport, how he'd said his immaculately tailored suit was his most comfortable.

Vladyr gives me a small nod, and I let out a whimper as I press my mouth to the tip of his cock. He's just soft enough in all the spaces that matter.

He strokes my hair gently as I drag my lips, my tongue, up and down the length of him, hard and hot and ready. I take the tip into my mouth, warming up my jaw, and he hisses in pleasure.

I take in more, greedily, as much as I can, my enamels be damned, and use my hands for what I can't fit in my mouth. I slide my hands up his thunderous thighs, cupping and stroking his sack with one hand and running my fingers up and down the base of his cock, tracing the veins. Within moments I find what I'm looking for. I tease the little bumps down the center of his shaft, his cock twitches against the roof of my mouth and the sound of him trying to hold back a groan fills the room.

I can't get enough of every little reaction, his heavy breaths, the way he shifts his hips, his wings twitching and his tail flicking involuntarily. I save every little movement and sound from him, wanting to preserve it in my memory forever.

The muscles in my jaw ache from how big he is in my mouth; how heavy he is against my tongue. I don't know how much longer I can do this for, with this much.

Tears burn in the corners of my eyes, and I feel his fingers run underneath my chin, lifting my gaze to his. He pulls his cock from my mouth and brushes the tip against my work-swollen lips. I lick at the bead of cum welling up in his slit, eliciting a groan from him.

I nearly forget myself at the taste of his cum. There's an earthiness to it, not quite as salty as I might have thought. The part of me that can smell something like rain on pavement from his kisses becomes ravenous for it. I've starved myself for so long, and it would be so simple to finally sate myself.

I nearly whimper at how much I want to stroke him until he finishes, but I also want to draw this out, to savor this night as much as I can.

He wipes a smudge of saliva from the corner of my lips as I savor the taste of him in my tired, achy mouth.

"Good girl," he murmurs, and claims my startled gasp with his mouth like a prize.

My cheeks flush warm and happy with his words. It makes my insides trill with delight and the need for my body to be used rises up in full force. When I break from the kiss for air, I whine and move back on the bed, laying back upon my elbows.

He parts my legs gently, his massive, clawed hands not scratching my skin in the slightest. He dips his head to deeply inhale, and I whimper. I'm already so wet I can feel it.

His long, pointed tongue traces against the heated skin of my inner thigh, setting off every nerve in my nethers.

"Vlad," I moan, begging for more, for anything at all.

I gasp, my back arching up off the bed as his tongue drags through my folds, hot against my clit, before delving deep within me. In another universe, I was probably having a thought about how non-soundproof hotel walls were; but in this one, only after my moans and keens of keep-doing-that-please did I realize I was not remotely containing my noises of pleasure.

"Vlad, Vladdy. I want you in me," I whine, unabashed to sound so needy for it, that I could somehow still need more than the feel of his tongue impossibly hot against my vulva as he licks hard, long strokes up the entirety of my slit.

Fuck it, I'll die by getting dicked down. It'll be good. That's probably how I was meant to go anyway.

"I will fuck you when you're ready for it," he snarls before he buries his tongue deep inside me, searing hot and reaching a lot farther than any tongue I've ever had in me. His massive hands slide beneath me to cup my ass, to lift my hips higher than I could to his mouth, my ankles landing over each of his shoulders.

My first orgasm takes me quickly, almost by surprise, with little build my nethers are left twitching and spasming. My legs are still visibly shuddering when he drags two huge fingers through the wetness of my cunt, then pressing deep into me. I can only moan weakly as he enters me, curling his fingers in just the right spot. I feel like putty in his hands, shaping into something that will fit around him.

He pulls his fingers out, and it leaves me empty and wanting.

There are a few moments to breathe and recover and mourn the absence of his tongue and fingers, as he surveys me, boneless and strewn naked across his bed. He brushes a finger against my calf, a gesture so gentle it might break me.

The bed shifts under me and pitches downwards under his weight as he puts one knee on the edge of the mattress, and then the other, moving forward to meet me. He sits on his heels, his thick, stony cock swaying heavily with the movements as he settles in.

"Are you ready?" he murmurs, taking my hips in his massive hands again. He spreads my legs wide, dragging my body up to meet his. My thighs all but straddle his cock, confirming to me that I was right about how unlikely it was I'd be able to take him.

"Yes, please," I nearly beg. Still, I hold my breath for the first time his cock head presses against my entrance and pushes in.

Every inch is an experience in patience and testing my limits, as I roll my hips to take in more of him, to find that satisfying friction. He's buffeting most of his thrusts against the bedframe, letting the furniture take the brunt of each motion.

I can see the flicker of pleasure that escapes his stony face, the restraint tensing in his muscles as he shifts in and out of me, easing me open. Each thrust deeper into me grazes a boundary, flirting with the point of pain, but never actually touching it. Every flirtation arcs into near satisfaction, twisting into wanting more as he pulls back again.

The bed cracks beneath us, pitching out from under me. The sound is startling, but Vlad pays no other attention to it other than to scoop me up off the bed so that I don't tumble away with it.

Vlad is just so massive compared to me that as he crouches down, it's nothing for him to hold my ankles open wide, hefting my hips into the air over my head, fucking into me like I'm just a toy upon his thick cock. Every movement brings me ass-over-head, as he thrusts down into me, fucking me into the mattress like he's going to bury me here.

The sensation of it is so much, I lose time. My next climax finds me quickly, each slam of his pelvis into mine tips me over the edge again, hard. Vladyr comes with a growl, his claws dig into the mattress, shredding bedding around me. His release is hot inside me, I can feel each spurt, each wave move through me. It feels truly endless, my orgasm wrenching pleasure out of every last molecule, and his filling me up, seeping through every crevice his cock hasn't filled.

He pulls his cock from me, and the last twitching spurts of cum paint my belly up to my tits. I drag my fingers through it, cooling rapidly, testing the way it becomes tacky between them.

I start to doze off, spent. The broken bed shifts under me, as he climbs onto the side next to me, curling a wing around us, even though we're alone.

It's cozier under there. I could easily fall asleep if I wasn't an utter mess. But before I can get up, I see he has a damp washcloth in hand.

Vlad nods to me and makes a gesture that I should lay back. "Let me take care of it," he murmurs.

Oh no. He's going to spoil me. And fuck, I want to let him.

I stretch, exhausted and satisfied, laying there lazily, letting him drag a damp cloth over my body.

His fingers draw it down to my cunt, messy and slick and dripping with his seed. Each pass he makes with the cloth brings him to brush against my oversensitive clit, still raw from his attentions, and it makes me squirm in his grip. A little more attention and I'll be coming again in his arms.

"No gold star?" I ask, and his response is a low chuckle that I can feel rumble in his chest against me. I know I'll be well sated by the end of this night.

But this is it. What happens on the work trip stays on the work trip.

14

Sitting next to Vlad, the last eight hours of presentations fly by. I wish I'd been sitting next to him from the start.

I can't help but keep looking over my shoulder, to see if anyone spots the way we're just a little bit cozier during the meetings than we had been before. Every now and then he knocks my shoulder with his and murmurs a joke or observation in my ear, and I try not to giggle like a schoolgirl or touch my knee against his too often. Does it look like we're flirting to anyone else?

It's fine. I doubt anyone suspects that we did anything we shouldn't have been doing. Even if I have to keep correcting my body language from leaning into his space every few minutes.

At the end of all the presentations, when everyone is packing their things up, Vlad hands me a sheet of something that glints in the low light. When I hold it closer to my face and squint, I find the metallic outline of little stars.

I bite down against a smile.

"Aren't you going to award me one?"

"I think you've earned the whole sheet," he murmurs back.

"Does that mean you've lowered the bar?" I tease, peeling one off. "I don't know that they go with my outfit."

"Then you should put it somewhere it won't clash," he returns, and I feel warm all over at the suggestion.

"Only if you find it later," I tease, before I remember I can't really offer that.

Our other coworkers are gathering one last time in front of the hotel, and we smile at each other and put another step of distance between ourselves.

It's the last night of the trip, and that fact makes my chest feel weirdly tight. I couldn't wait for it to be over just a few days ago. I had been dreading this whole event for the months leading up to it.

And now . . . I don't know what I want.

It's not like I don't miss my own bed. And being able to go hours and hours alone, undisturbed. Pretending to pay attention to everything that has nothing to do with my department is like having a second full time job.

I try to convince myself that I'm just dreading going back to my actual job after doodling my way through all day PowerPoint presentations and getting nothing done.

That's it.

That's all.

There's a ferry to take us down the river to dinner, though some of the more motion sickness prone members of our company figured out a carpool option to get to the restaurant. After about two minutes on the boat, I'm kind of wishing I took that option. It's crowded and chilly and I have to listen to Deanna loudly telling Soven how she used to be a bodybuilder. I only tune in occasionally when I get bored of staring at the water, and I'm not sure if she means in the competitive way or the necromancy way.

Every so often, I glance at Vlad across the ferry and get a smile or cheesy wink from him. I have to fight against a smile. There hasn't been a real moment alone with Vlad since we slept together, and it's actively torturing me.

Which doesn't make sense. It's been long enough by now, and after that night in his hotel room, my needs should be sated. Really, I think I should have had enough Vitamin D to last a lifetime, but even looking at him now still makes my cheeks warm.

The ferry arrives at some fancy boathouse place—I didn't catch the name when Lily announced it. I follow the tide of people.

It's a little bit nice, I concede internally, *to get to spend time with all of them and chat about nothing in particular.*

"Alright party people, are you ready to join me in your personal empowerment?" a woman calls into a microphone, greeting us in a flair of flowing purple robes and a hood that obscures most of her face.

Kathy glances at me. "They can't be serious. They got a speaker from the Cult of Productivity?"

"Gotta end all the corporate enthusiasm with a bang."

"It's not a cult, it's team building," Lily interjects as she shimmies past us, and jogs in heels over towards one of the boathouse staff members with her clipboard in hand.

"Cult of Team Building, then," I correct Kathy. She rolls her eyes at me but sticks by my side as we follow the drift of people into the building, which opens immediately into a large, wide room with a high ceiling.

It kind of reminds me of a ballroom if only a little too plain. It's got that "any event can be held here" vibe that doesn't photograph as well as you'd hope. Still, there are some balloons filling the space, some tables on one side of the room, a little bar set up in the corner. The empty space and speakers on the other side of the room make me a little apprehensive. I don't know who in their right might planned this and really thought they'd be able to get any of their coworkers to boogie.

Kathy heads straight for the bar, and since I've kind of attached my will to be social to her, I follow. I order whatever she's having and try not to show too plainly that it tastes vile.

We do that thing we're so good at when we hang out, which is not talk at all, staring around the room for long stretches of time. We watch our coworkers pick at an hors d'oeuvres spread and loosen up after a few drinks. The music kicks on, way louder than it needs to be, and yet the Cult of Productivity lady is louder.

She keeps asking in an overly dramatic voice, "Are you going to be a part of the problem or a part of the solution, people?"

"Well, we can't have solution people without problem people," Kathy sniffs, trying to maneuver her cup around her beak.

"You're a vital part of the economy, really."

"It's really important that we make problems even harder than they were to start with."

I hold back my remark that she's getting a little too close to reality.

"I'll put your file in the shredder if you actually say any of that to her," I offer with just a hint of jest. I kinda mean it.

"But I worked so hard on that!"

I roll my eyes at her, and they land on Vlad again, because the cultist has managed to corner him next.

She's been going around in her long purple robes introducing herself to everyone and spending a lot of time chatting with people about their career paths, what they see for themselves in the future. She has a lot to say about maximizing our morning rituals, highlighting the ways we all could be doing more.

Yeah, of course he knows all that nonsense, he's tired of it, I roll my eyes on his behalf. I hope he gives her a run for her money.

We move along when the cultist gets a little too close to us, and when we've circled the room at least once, I ask Kathy, "Where's Ted?"

"Over there," she answers without even looking, tilting her head to a corner of the ballroom. "We have to go back to normal at some point, don't we?"

As she says this, I glance back to Vlad, and my whole body ignites when I see him looking at me with those dark amber eyes. I have to hold myself back from running away from this conversation and to him. My hands dig into the nearest tablecloth, and I only get a few inches before the weight of the plates on it anchors me down.

It makes me sad to think we won't even see each other at work because we're in different offices. We might email every once in a while, or call and chat. It won't be the same as being right there with him, though. Still, maybe we could meet up in person every now and then for a reprise.

I hang nearby, hoping to catch some of his conversation, but the music's too loud to hear Vlad's low, soothing voice. I stay in place a little too long, trying to listen. After a few minutes, I make out just enough to realize he's talking about volunteering at a local undead sanctuary.

"There's been a huge influx of new visitors after the whole Dark Regime change up," Vlad is saying as I inch closer." . . . I was asking Angela if she would help with a class-action suit the shelter was preparing. There was a typo in the contract. Now instead of souls damned to eternity, it's soup. It's been a mess trying to renegotiate."

I never knew to ask him about that. My heart swells to think that's he's such a sweet guy he would spend his little free time volunteering, that there's still so much about him I don't know and wish I did. But at the same time, it sinks a little in me. Of course, he's got causes to champion and support, he's got his life together.

I'm so lost in thought, I barely notice when Kathy jogs off in the other direction, and someone replaces her on my other side in a swoosh of purple.

I catch sight of Vlad nearby, and for a moment I think maybe it's him, with his bluish-gray wings. But he's still too far away.

Then I see the cult woman is absent from his side, and at mine.

Her smile is wide with a few too many teeth as she grabs my hand and tries to professionally break it. I don't think humans are supposed to have that many teeth, but I'm not entirely sure. She uses her grip to tow me back over to where she was talking to Vlad, and there's a pinch of panic in my chest that I'm in trouble. That's not really possible, because she doesn't have any authority over us.

"Hi, I'm Jenna, the guru from the Productivity Empowerment New Initiative Seminar. I'm here to teach everyone at Evil Inc. how to maximize their goals."

"Oh! Wow. That's a mouthful. I'm, uh, Gwen, I'm in Monster Resources," I stammer, and feel already a little lost. I didn't know goals could be maximized, and I'm a little scared to learn what that means.

"Vladyr was just telling me about you," she tells me, and he does seem to still be a part of this conversation.

"Guilty," he shrugs, and gives me an apologetic smile from over her shoulder. Clearly, he didn't realize that Jenna was looking for victims. "I was just telling her about your unlimited PTO idea."

Something of a playful urge rises in me. The minute she looks away from me, I'm going to get him back for this.

I take a deep breath and look at the cult lady. Until the opportunity shows itself, I just need to survive this conversation.

Truthfully, I'd been avoiding her because I was sure she's going to tell me to cut out all the little ways I slack off and hold myself more accountable, but I can make the best of this. Maybe she could give me some pointers and my little idea could become an actual plan.

She takes a different course of action than I expect, and starts with, "So, what are your retention rates?"

I blink. "What?"

"Your company's retention rates, or turnover, or . . . "

She's looking at me and expecting me to produce an actual number while I have a mixed drink in my hand. I glance between her and Vlad a few times to check that she's serious. All I get is a raised brow from Vlad and an expectant look from her, before weakly responding, "Um, I'm not a hiring manager."

This barely slackens her inquisition. "Well, what about the employee engagement statistics? Training and development?"

"I don't have any of that off the top of my head," I start to tell her, and start to gesture to the rest of the ballroom where everyone else seems to be in the middle of enjoying themselves.

"That's no excuse," she gasps at me like I've offended her. Suddenly, it's like I'm back in school, and there's a test that I was supposed to be better prepared for.

Did she grill everyone else like this? I don't see anyone else as distressed as I feel though, and that makes me wonder if I'm the only one this level of unprepared. I flail internally, trying not to crumple.

I look to Vlad for help, but he's watching me like he's also waiting for my answer. Does he expect me to just know these kinds of things all the time? Maybe that's just the standard he works to.

It's clear then that they both see right through me. I've always known that all my rambling about being up to date on the relevant topics in my field means nothing, because I don't have a degree in this. While I may be able to get through the paperwork and the meetings, I don't have any real expertise to offer.

"I gotta run to the bathroom, I'll be right back," I mumble, handing my drink to Vlad and leaving before either of them can say anything. I don't care that I'm kind of obviously fleeing.

I duck into the hallway for a moment, closing my eyes and rubbing my temples. Deep breaths. The thunderous music still seeps in under the doors, thrumming in time with my rapid pulse.

I can tuck this existential dread away for later. As much as it brings my mood down, it's nothing I haven't already known about myself. And maybe I had a couple fun days pretending like I operate on the same level of organization and competency as everyone else, but it's time to come back to reality, as much as it crushes my ego to do so.

There isn't much time to shake it off. The microphone screeches with feedback as someone tests it out.

"It's time for office trivia!" the cult speaker announces with way too much energy, her voice competing with the too-loud music. "I hope you're cozy enough with your coworkers to know all the answers!"

Maybe she rattled me a little, but I can get back in there. Everyone has started moving towards the round tables set up with folding chairs around them.

I catch sight of Vlad on the far side of the room, looking around, my drink still in his hand. It would be so easy to go over there and try to play off all that, explain my lack of experience and knowledge with a quick joke about the drinks here being too strong.

I force myself to look away. I need to start tapering off from him. When we all go home, we're not going to see any more of each other.

A few of the usual suspects are gathering nearby; Jessica, Bill, and Deanna all sit around one of the tables. Jessica seems to be fitting in well, talking about adjusting to having her own desk. I end up slipping into a chair next to Bill, looking a little more undead than usual. It's been a hot minute since I had a personal conversation with anyone, but last corporate retreat I just kept letting him tell me about his hobbies and explain how to do sudoku a bunch of times.

"So. Um. Do you still play sudoku?"

"A little bit, I've been taking a break since I got stuck on a hard puzzle. I think it always helps to look at something with fresh eyes," he starts to tell me, but his creaky, ancient voice is quickly overwhelmed by Deanna's loud chatter.

"Well, this is Gwen's first real job too, isn't it?"

I look over when I hear my name and frown. That's not really a fact I want everyone to know. My teeth start to weld to themselves as I try to smile and shrug through the conversation.

Jessica's vague form leans toward me for a second, her void making curious sounds. "I think you told me a while back, you were a temp in the Peak District?"

"No, no, she *tempted* in the Peaks," Deanna interrupts, before I can say anything. Deanna nudges me good-naturedly, and winks, "That is what you meant when you said what you were doing was soul-sucking, right?"

She clearly thinks she's funny. She must be because the others laugh.

And I have never felt smaller.

15

Well, now I just don't want to hang out with these people.

I don't mask it quickly enough, a flicker of my thoughts must show briefly on my face, because Deanna catches it, leans closer to me with her wide smile, and nudges me with her elbow.

"Just teasing, baby girl," she assures me, doing nothing to actually stem the adrenaline coursing through me. My heart is pounding. Well, if she's just teasing, then of course it's nothing.

I glance at the rest of our coworkers, the way they're staring back at me, watching for the slightest change in their expressions, if they're looking at me differently now than they were a moment ago. I didn't even realize Deanna knew. How could she have known? I never told anyone.

But I guess Vlad had put it together himself without me telling him, others must have been able to. And even if they hadn't, Deanna just did.

This moment feels like it's being trapped in amber. I watch the opportunity to say something, to cut her joke down for what it is, flutter away while my courage fails to rise.

I don't have it in me.

"Of course," I nod, and shrug it off, pretending my heart doesn't close like a fist around her words.

I put on a pinched smile for as long as I can, and when the attention finally shifts to someone else, and they're all laughing again, I quietly slip away from the table.

When I step outside, the din falls away quickly. As soon as the door falls shut behind me, it mutes the sounds of the party almost entirely. It's cooler out on the veranda, and as I inhale deeply, I realize how shaky my breath is in my throat. I settle against the veranda's railing.

My smile fades as realization sets in. I really convinced myself that no one knew, that I could keep the important, vulnerable things to myself. And I thought that maybe people liked me here.

I go through the eight stages of grief in the expanse of a few seconds. The alcohol helps, honestly. Maybe that's why these trips are so quick to have it readily available—all these people who don't actually like each other all that much, pretending to get along so they can get through another day with their paycheck intact.

"Hey, Team Player."

I didn't realize I wasn't alone. I look up before I realize I know this voice. Vlad followed me out here, I don't know exactly when. Maybe I was too caught up in my feelings to notice the door opening again.

A rattled laugh escapes me. Yeah, that would be what it looks like. I'm running away from the party because I can't stand being around other people, because that's a weird little me thing, and not because people at large are terrible.

"Hey, yourself. I see you're, um, also lurking," I fumble for cheeriness, for words that won't break me to say. I don't want to bring what just happened inside out here with me, I don't want him to know about any of it.

"Taking a quick break before I dive back into the cult initiation," he says easily, pushing off the wall and crossing to me. It's hard to not just lean into his side, to draw too close for coworkers to be.

Deanna's little comment had eclipsed that earlier panic attack, I'd nearly forgotten about it. Silver lining or something, until he'd reminded me about it.

"Yeah, it's kind of intense in there. I didn't think you were going to ambush me like that," I say, crossing my arms, my voice coming out a little too harsh. I keep trying to school my posture, my face, into something less outwardly panicked and aggressive, but my composure keeps slipping. My body wants to shift into something more ferocious, like a cat's tail becoming all bushy.

"I thought you worked in the Peaks," he frowns. "You know how it goes in a pitch session."

I wilt, my teeth crushing the words, *I was just an intern*. I never pitched anything except everyone's empty coffee cups into the trash.

My silence is just as frosty as anything I'm holding back, it seems. His expression softens with concern, his wings drifting inwards.

"I'm sorry I ambushed you like that. I thought I was giving you a chance to practice your unlimited PTO proposal. But that really wasn't the way to help, was it?"

Some of my roiling emotions diffuse at his apology, some of them only complicate. I know he means well, that he was trying to help in his own way. But we have such different ideas of what that looks like.

I don't really know how I feel about being out here with him. There's no one else I would rather see right now, but at the same time, right now I don't want to be seen at all.

"I can't wait to get in my own bed at home," I say, even though I don't mean a word of it. I just want to dive into his arms and hold him and not have to think about the rest of the world. "This whole trip has just gone on so long, and I've had enough of these people to last me a lifetime."

It veers a little too close to what I'm actually feeling, and a hitch of emotion poisons my casual tone.

It doesn't escape Vlad. He glances behind us, at the glassy doors. He takes my hand and pulls me out of their view, a little way down the veranda. I don't have the energy to stop the way the simple movement brings me closer to him, gently corralled into his space. His wings tuck around us, providing a small sense of privacy.

"For what it's worth, I'm glad you came with us tonight," he smiles at me, and I can see he really is proud of me. It hurts as much as it feels good, but I don't know that I can handle both feelings layered on top of one another right now. "That first night I didn't think you'd ever come out of your shell."

"Pssh! I don't have a shell," I roll my eyes. I'm here, aren't I? Pretending to be friendly and outgoing as well as competent.

"Your shell is the envy of all hermit crabs," he says, dipping his head to kiss the space between my neck and shoulder. "I think everything I've learned about you, I've had to convince you to share with me."

I wrinkle my nose reflexively. "That's not true."

Exhausted, I let myself truly crumple against him. It's safe. He's safe. If it were up to me, he would wrap his wings around us for the rest of the night, and we would just stay out here.

"Let's see . . . you should probably be taking some time off," he teases, and looking up at him in his arms, I'm kind of glad I didn't.

"I think that's your personal observation," I return. "Not a hard-hitting fact."

He presses a kiss to the top of my head, and it's so sweet, I swear I can feel it all the way down to my toes. Maybe ten more of those will cure everything that ails me, or maybe they'll hollow me out with the need for an endless amount of them.

"Oh, believe me, I've got facts too," he presses on, a hint of a smile in his voice.

I prepare to hear him tell me a list of boring tangible things, like my height.

"You advocate for everyone but yourself. You're passionate about making work environments more hospitable, and you're talented. You bring an admirable level of patience to the people around you."

There is an overwhelming urge to flee.

"Wow. I think that's almost enough to steal my identity," I joke, hoping the humor will provide me with some kind of escape hatch. Honestly, what I wouldn't give to have my identity stolen about ten minutes ago. "I'm not sure if you think I have a praise kink or if you're really bad at it."

He chuckles, but ignores my skepticism. "Maybe a praise kink would make it easier to accept it. I think it's a rare and compassionate person who actually puts people first in your job. Anyone else would have had a lot less patience for Kathy and Ted's particular relationship."

I feel held by him, and not just literally. Beheld, perhaps. Like he sees me unequivocally, without any of the mess or distraction of the little things.

And for some reason, that only intensifies the unease in my stomach. My throat feels uncomfortably tight.

I'm quiet for too long, maybe he thinks I've accepted his assertions as fact. I don't know what I've done to make him think any of that, or how to begin to correct it.

"There's an age-old urge to . . . climb the highest peaks. To claim the biggest mountain as my perch, and bring my mate there," he murmurs, his voice so low it reverberates through him like a purr.

I pause and blink at this gargoyle. It's such a vast change in topic, for a moment I'm not sure I'm actually keeping up.

I frown. "Your mate?"

"Someone to take back to my lair, share our lives together."

"You have a lair?" I wrinkle my nose and, yes, deflect. I need just a little more to figure out what exactly I missed.

"It's a timeshare," he shrugs, before giving his head a little shake, and making a verbal U-turn out of that line of inquiry. "Gwen . . . it'd be nice to see you around there sometime."

I watch the way his wings shift around us, opening just enough to frame the night sky reflecting into the water. I can't help but wonder if the view from his lair has twice as many stars.

I halt in his grasp, identifying one of the many fluttering sensations going on in my abdomen, realizing how it differs from the usual in-heat ones. It's too soft, too achy, too fragile and hopeful. As much as I need this trip to end, I don't want to see him go, I want to spend more time with him, as much time as I can.

It would never work.

Him being a gargoyle, he's probably centuries old. Not exactly my age bracket. And yeah, he's big and broad and stoic and nice and really just a bit of a nerd.

But there's a reason I would never go back to work in the Peaks. It's nothing but seeking out corporate power. Admittedly, I don't know what the dating and or mating scene is like for gargoyles, but I can only imagine he'd want a mate that would be that same high-powered, high achiever type. Not someone who doesn't have her shit together.

It feels wrong in my gut. I know he's not like that, everything we've ever talked about, every moment we've been alone together has shown me that. But I know I'm still wrong for him.

Clearly, I've fooled him into thinking we have something here. It wasn't on purpose. I mean, I like him a lot. I like him so much. He's been nothing but kind and understanding towards me, but the person he thinks I am doesn't exist. He doesn't know the slacker me, the person I am most of the time; the greasy, wearing yesterday's dirty clothes every day for weeks, with a vibrator propped up on my laptop's keyboard typing gibberish on an empty document so that my icon always shows as "BUSY" so I can play video games during work.

I know what's good for me, and it would be to crush this feeling with my bare hands. Fragile as the sensation is, I'm powerless to do anything to destroy it.

I can only hold it hostage in me, while it gouges my heart from the inside out.

My hands tighten into fists at my sides, holding on to my resolve. How did "What happens on work trips stays on work trips" eclipse not sleeping with a coworker in my brain?

"Yeah. Yeah, maybe we could. And we could keep it casual. Business casual, even. Business casual with benefits," I ramble, looking hopefully at him. But I can feel myself physically backing away before the railing meets my back.

"I don't think those words make sense in the way you're thinking they do," he says, and his brow pinches in confusion. It's not the response he wanted, but he hides his disappointment well. "I understand if you don't want to . . ."

My heart aches terribly for him. I really like him. I'd love to be able to simply dive into what he's offering, but I can't claim the credit he gives me. How horrible, that Vlad would offer something so vulnerable as a corner of his heart to me, and I can't receive it?

"No, I do, I just . . ." the words dry up before I can say them. It's already hard enough to refuse his offer, but to reveal how utterly unworthy of it I am? It's all I have left of us. The thought makes my throat close up and tears creep out onto my eyelashes, threatening to show themselves.

"I'm sorry, I can't do this right now."

"Are you ok? Did something happen?"

I shake my head, my teeth welding together. If I tell him, he's just going to want to fix it, when there's nothing to fix. It can't go back to the way I thought it was, and I was living in a fantasy if I thought people just kind of ignored me instead of actively gossiping about me behind my back.

"Gwen, it's clear you're upset."

Somehow, those words pierce me more than anything else—that I can't muscle through a difficult conversation without my feelings becoming transparent.

"No, I just want to be alone. I shouldn't have come here tonight. I think I'm just going to go back to the hotel. I'll get a cab," I blather, verbally scrambling for something that will let me escape this conversation.

I try to turn away, and I see the way his wings flex, him holding back the urge to curl them around me and hold me there with him. In some small part, I wish he'd just do that. If only there were no more talking, and just holding. But, of course, it can't be that simple.

"I can see what you're doing."

I stop in my tracks, feeling his eyes on me. "I don't know what you mean."

"It's one thing if you don't want to deal with me, it's another that you keep hiding yourself away from anyone who could possibly begin to care about you."

My breath stops in my throat. I've never felt so bare in front of him.

He takes my stillness as an opportunity to brush the back of his hand against mine. Not holding me, just barely touching. "I can see the way you keep hiding bits of yourself away so that people won't hurt you, but you deprive yourself of the chance to be appreciated. You have so much to express, and you won't let anyone see it."

"Vlad," I plead, swallowing hard, staring at the ground.

"Gwen," he says softly, and shifts his grasp so he can hold me in the tenderness of his gaze. "You are so immensely good at what you do."

"STOP IT."

The words leave my mouth in a snap, a screech. They're too hard, too biting. I pull my hand away. I can't bring myself to meet his eyes again, but I watch the stillness of his tail.

He's building me up, and I can't let him do that. I need him to stop raising his expectations for what I'm capable of, because I can't even reach the bar where it's currently at.

"I don't need your help, or your guidance. I don't need someone to placate me with empty affirmations. You don't know *anything* about me."

It comes out venomous.

I can't help it. There are tears rolling down my cheeks as I grit my teeth together and try to hold them back. My hands are clenched fists that I can't pry open, so I wipe the tears away on the back of my wrists.

It's not until I'm breathing ragged in the silence from how viciously I'd hissed at him, that I realize what I've said.

Vlad holds my gaze, but slowly nods. His eyes search my face, but he doesn't press for more. His wings recede, tucking close behind him.

"I should, um, go. I have some emails to send," I say, even as my brain stutters to reconcile what I'm doing. I don't know when, if ever, I'm going to see him again, but somehow that feels as right as it does wrong. I emotionally clock out right there and then.

I don't remember if I smiled and nodded and told him how nice it was to meet him on this trip, or if I turned on my heel and left the place without another word.

16

Which of these things should you not say to a coworker?

A) Good Morning

B) Did you get a new haircut?

C) How was your weekend?

D) Remember when we hooked up in that phone closet?
Thinking of you.

I stare at the screen, only taking in how much worse this is going to be with the upbeat generic corporate music that plays in the background when employees take the quiz.

I hit the backspace key until the last answer clears and rub my forehead. I haven't been able to think of anything that isn't something I would say to Vlad if I emailed him.

We've emailed back and forth a little since the retreat ended and work resumed as normal. Nothing more than necessary. It's all overly professional and stilted because of how we left things.

After forwarding so many of Kathy and Ted's email threads to him, I can type out v.grotesce@evil.co.com faster than most of my passwords, and the muscle memory carries me through entering the address. I want to talk to Vlad, even if I don't really know what to say after I yelled at him.

It's bad enough when it's someone I can quietly cut out of my life when things inevitably go sour, but somehow, it's worse that it's the gargoyle I kept bumping into and making a fool of myself in front of, then drunkenly kissed, and was completely ready to jump his bones. It's kind of a leap in topics from the MR paperwork.

But life goes on after work trips.

My plants are looking a little peckish, having not been watered for a week, but that's about all that's changed. I work from home, playing an endless stream of podcasts and movies and anything that will keep me from being alone with my thoughts. I really want to go somewhere, but I don't know where. I just know I am so tired of keeping myself company.

I end up going to the office of my own volition, for once.

Well, sort of. I could just call Kathy about the new complaint she's filing instead of scheduling a one-on-one meeting with her, but I need the change of pace. My apartment has become a black hole of despair that is actually starting to get to me.

Some part of me hopes, when I get there, that nothing will have changed. That maybe everything that happened could stay packed away as a distant memory.

Waiting for the meeting room to empty, I hover by the water cooler alone, and rest my paper cup against it, pretending it's not weird to just stand somewhere, doing nothing.

For the most part, no one really notices, people I don't talk to just pass me by without a look. My shoulders start to untense until I spy a familiar three pens tucked into a little blonde bun zipping past.

"Afternoon, Gwen, I heard you had to go home early last week, everything alright?" Lily asks, just as I'm registering that it's her.

"I, uh. Yeah. I wasn't feeling well," I lie, and shrug a little.

"Aw, well I hope you're feeling better," she gives me a sympathetic frown. She's always been nice. For a moment, I think maybe it's not as bad as I've built it up in my head.

We don't get a chance to talk much more, as the meeting room's door opens and most of the HR department start to leave. Lily waves one of the humans over.

Janice just barely conceals the way she instantly recoils upon seeing me. I hold myself still and try not to react, wishing desperately in that moment that I'd never left the apartment.

It is as bad as I'd thought. Everyone knows I'm a soul-sucking siren, and I shouldn't have hoped otherwise.

"See you later," Lily says, and flounces away as she always does before I get a chance to respond.

I slip into the emptied meeting room. It's amazing how a job can go from kind of nice to something I dread, not because of the work itself but the people I have to be with.

But it is just a job. A job I have to keep doing, at the moment, if nothing else. I'll have to hold onto it a bit longer while I look for something else, at least.

Why does it have to be so hard to get to know people? I either have to feel like I'm deceiving people by hiding my nature, or "be myself" like some trite, after-school special would tell me to, and basically invite them to become gross, awful versions of themselves. Why can't it just be easy?

Kathy cracks open the door and seems to internally curse that I've gotten there before her. She holds me in her stare for a long moment, almost daring me to bring up what I witnessed her and Ted doing last week in the elevator.

It would be easy to bring it up like she's a petulant child who needs to learn how to behave, instead of treating her like an adult who has her own reasons for the decisions she makes. Whether those reasons are good or bad, is not for me to judge.

"I'm still catching up on unpacking, from the trip," I say, more to break the silence than anything else.

"Yeah, I think I left a couple things behind," she says, watching me carefully.

I nod and try not to think of leaving Vlad on the balcony. I close my eyes and I swear I can see him still standing there, the dejected slant of his shoulders, his tail resting against the ground. I opt for sighing something pointless instead. "I . . . always leave at least one sock under the hotel bed."

She offers a little laugh and sits down across from me, stretching comfortably in the seat.

"So, tell me what Ted did this time," I say, hefting their file onto the table, getting out a pen.

"Ted? No, this one's about Deanna."

I almost drop my pen. "What?"

Kathy shrugs, and starts combing out the feathers on her arm, shedding little bits of dust and fluff onto the meeting room table. "I thought Deanna was out of line. Put in a complaint about her. Lied a little, for funsies."

"You can't do that," I start to say, but she interrupts.

"Well, you weren't going to," she says, as if this much is obvious. "I was there, and I don't know why you just laughed along with her. That was a fucked up thing to say to anyone."

Honestly, I'm speechless. A little touched, even. But I can't overlook the fact that she really, really, can't do that. "That may be, but—"

"Come on, I clearly know my way around a complaint form. Besides, it's a smack on the wrist. Just to rattle her," Kathy pleads, before she offers in a hushed tone, "Unless you want me to do more."

"Kathy, no."

"I can move all the furniture in her office two inches out of its normal spot. Sabotage her filing system. Sprinkle crumbs in her carpet so she gets ants."

"I appreciate what you're trying to do, but I'm not going to file that."

"I don't think you do," she grumbles, sinking low in her seat. She kicks at the ground and swivels the chair back-and-forth a bit. "What's the point of having friends if I can't lie for them?"

Rubbing my temples, I lean back in my chair and sigh. I have a feeling if I gave her a little more leeway, she'd start signing Deanna's email up for a bunch of time-sucking webinars and newsletters. She's done it to Ted plenty of times.

It's a little hard not to smile though. It's sweet of her to try. When provoked, she easily starts bringing a certain "we should all walk out" vibe to the workplace that no doubt upper management is a little wary of. With enough momentum, I can imagine her unionizing the Dark Regime.

After a moment, a thought crosses my mind that makes the breath in my chest ache. "Did he put you up to this?"

"Who, Ted?" Kathy glances up and immediately scoffs. "Ted's an ass. Don't give him credit for anything, ever."

I hold back any comment about her being all over that particular ass just last week, and simply shake my head. "Never mind. Um. How do you like having a new boss?"

"He's ok," she shrugs, continuing to sprawl out of the swivel chair. "It's nice to have a boss that cares. I don't love it though, because I feel bad about procrastinating, and I'm not about that."

I nod, and we lapse into silence. She nods as well, feeling the quiet a little too intently.

"How's work, otherwise?" I ask, with no real intent to listen.

It pinches in my chest to think about Vlad, to want to pry for more information. But doing so would unearth everything we had put away when the trip was over. I shouldn't linger over Vlad's words, the way he believed in a better version of me than really existed. The way he wanted me to believe in that version, even after I'd rejected his feelings.

I couldn't have ever accepted them, as much as I wanted to. I did the right thing. He would have learned sooner or later how I didn't live up to his expectations, and breaking my heart then would have just hurt all the more for it.

But somehow, I hated the thought of pushing him away more.

"So, Miguel's taking a longer leave, and we're down a person on the next big tradeshow," Kathy is rambling when I remember to nod along. "On top of that, there's extra badges, but the event coordinators won't refund it. And now Vlad is trying to see if we can get some of our people to go, and they can at least make it seem like people are interested in visiting our tradeshow booth. But this soon after the last big work trip, I don't think we're gonna get any volunteers before tomorrow—"

"I'll go," falls out of my mouth before I truly process the words.

Kathy blinks at me, clearly expecting some other kind of response. Usually, I'm reliable for bemoaning the day-to-day trivialities of the job.

I swallow, and nod again. "If you need someone to show up, I'll be there. Just forward me the details, ok?"

"Yeah. I can do that," she shrugs. "It won't be as bad as the last trip. Lily and Janice are gonna be there too, they're ok. Well, I like Lily alright, and she always invites Janice. But she's never been a dick to me."

"Sounds like it'll be fun," I lie, a little deflated to remember Janice, and how she reacted when she saw me. Kathy might not care, but clearly some people are bothered by my presence alone, now that they know what I am. And for that much, I'm reminded that I was right to break things off with Vlad. Maybe I shouldn't have yelled or run away like that. But it had to be done.

My heart is still beating rapidly at the thought of seeing Vlad again, I'm not sure if it's dread or something else, when Kathy pushes away from the table, says some brief farewell as she heads out, that I return without thinking.

The impulse that moved me to speak still flutters hard in my chest. I want to see Vlad again, if only to apologize for how I ended things between us. He deserves that much. And perhaps selfishly, I want every second of him that I can have.

I open a drawer on my desk and brush a handful of paperclips into it haphazardly, stuffing the debris out of sight. If only it was that easy to stuff away the rest of my feelings. Everything he made me feel just by being around him and talking to him hasn't left me just because I'm alone now. It sits inside me, making it hard to fully breathe.

I leave work a little early to get to an appointment. The dentist's office is the first bit of unabridged quiet I've had since getting back home. There isn't even music playing in the waiting room. The silence weighs heavy on my chest.

Usually seeing Dr. Lucille isn't my favorite thing, because she's so chatty and overly friendly, and her hair snakes don't know the meaning of personal space. But there really isn't anyone else who takes my insurance in the area.

"Girl. What did I say about taking care of your enamels? Are you back to grinding your teeth again?" Dr. Lucille says while poking the little mirror tool in my mouth. I'm trying not to breathe in her face, but it's a little difficult while she's peering at my back molars.

She adds a little threat when I fail to answer, "Just look at these scrapes on them. I will send you home with a mouth guard."

"I'm not grinding my teeth," I say around her plastic-gloved fingers, but it still comes out a little garbled. She's probably used to it.

"Taking Abyssal lessons again?"

"Nmo," I reply, and accidentally lick her finger in the process of trying not to. One more thing to add to my list of reasons I need a break from existing.

"Hm," she says, and adjusts the overhead light. "Oh, look at this bruise."

"Wheh?"

"On your soft palette," she mutters, drawing the back of the mirror tool against the roof of my mouth to let me know where it is. She hums again, before presuming, "Aw, good for you, getting out of your house."

She takes her tools out of my mouth momentarily, landing in her little swivel stool and rolling back across the room to flip the page in my chart and glance at it.

I sit up and frown at her. "What do you mean?"

She cracks a wide smile and gestures at her own mouth, indicating the roof. "The blowjob bruise."

I don't have the energy to be scandalized that she can tell.

"Oh. Yeah," I mumble, and sit back in the chair. Distantly, it all kind of clicks into place, a mystery that didn't really need solving. "That's probably what scraped my enamels up."

"Oh. Well, I can set you up with a different kind of mouthguard for—" she says and looks too excited at the prospect of telling me how to protect my teeth against stone cocks for all the mouth-bruising fellatio I want.

"I don't need a mouth guard, I'm not going to see him again," I insist, cutting her off quickly. I really don't want to hear about it right now.

She nods and goes back to the manila folder with all my previous visit's records in it, making a note. She continues chatting over her shoulder. "I miss the days when it was just tooth keys and crushing teeth to bits. Now it's all X-rays and submitting health insurance paperwork."

She's gone on rambles about the good old Dark Reigns before, and usually that's my cue to nod along and say something about the weather and the state of the roads, to try to remember something I liked about the last century. But I can't. I can't hear a thing she's saying, because I'm thinking about everything I was holding at bay.

I told him no because I didn't want to get hurt. But now it hurts so much. I liked him so much; I couldn't bear the thought of what it would feel like to find the same disappointment with him I always feel when someone shows me their true colors.

I'm not about to be crying in my dentist's office over a guy I had an office fling with. I'm not. I'm really not.

I head to the front of the office, and Dr. Lucille's hair snakes flick their little tongues out goofily, trying to lift my mood with their own.

"Since you didn't bite me like my last patient did, I thought I'd let you take something from the treat bowl," she offers, a kind little gesture. I return a fraction of her smile and look into the plastic bowl full of sugar-free lollipops and glow in the dark keychains.

She shakes the bowl a little as she holds it out, and in the tumble of fun little nothings, a sheet of shiny, star-shaped stickers is unearthed.

And there goes my composure.

Tears slip down my face, and even as I brush the corner of my sleeves at them, more follow. I fight against the way the corners of my mouth pull down against my will, and then the first gasp shakes my body almost violently. It's loud and inevitable, and I can't do anything but let it happen, as much as I try to steel myself against it, to hold it back.

What was so awful about a guy who thought the world of me, that I had to go and ruin everything? I couldn't just say yes to what we both wanted, because I really thought so much of myself, that I had the ability to deceive everyone around me. If only I'd been simply able to trust his perspective.

The dentist offers an awkward little pat on my shoulder and a tissue box, and gives me a few moments to collect myself, before sending me off with a new toothbrush and floss samples.

17

Every minute that passes before the tradeshow, the more I feel like volunteering was a mistake. I keep feeling like I don't know why I'm doing this, even though I know I just want to apologize to Vlad in person. I can't think of a good way to duck out and run home that wouldn't leave me flinching in anxiety. Kathy has probably already told Vlad I'd show up. I'm sure half of the impetus for volunteering is just the weird leftover feelings from the company trip that's left me feeling off. I've been feeling weird since the middle of the trip, honestly. I have *always* preferred privacy and solitude.

At least, before Vlad, I thought I did.

Now I can't bear the thought of just going back to my empty apartment to wait for my heart to sew itself back together, sitting around in the quiet, restlessly flipping through channels and different apps, unable to concentrate on anything for more than a couple minutes but being unable to sit with just my thoughts as well.

Lily makes eye contact with me in the hotel lobby, which ends up being the thing that pulls me into the group. The carpool over to the tradeshow is quiet, with all of us mostly chewing our breakfast sandwiches. I'm glad, at least, that I squeezed in last and didn't end up sitting next to Janice, but when we get out of the car, I end up walking beside her to the venue.

"Hi," I try with a quick smile, but even that feels like a trespass.

She returns it weakly but offers nothing more.

"What's the company policy on getting reimbursed for tipping?" Kathy calls out, glancing at the rest of us as our ride departs, and she's tucking the receipt away in her purse.

"I don't think tips are part of what gets reimbursed."

"Oh, that's going in the complaint box."

Lily's brow wrinkles just the slightest bit. "You thought we had a complaint box? That's just for me."

Janice looks unamused as she finishes her breakfast. "Don't listen to her. She doesn't have as much power as she wants you to think."

"Shut up, I'm extremely powerful. I have spies and shit."

Janice rolls her eyes, and they land on me. It takes me a moment to realize she did that for my benefit. Maybe I'm supposed to gently tease Lily too, but the moment slips by as I don't know either of them well enough for that.

"Is it still weird?" Janice asks, glancing sidelong at me. The emotion passing through me feels like snagging a cashmere sweater on a hook and watching as it unravels. Lily eyes the pair of us like she's watching an opera, but doesn't comment.

"What do you mean?"

"I don't know, I guess I'm always going to be a little awkward around you," she admits a little sheepishly, and that snagged feeling of dread tangles in my stomach. ". . . You did have to handle my file for Monster Resources."

I blink. "You have a very small file. Nothing compared to this one," I say, tilting my head at Kathy, who preens like I gave her an award.

"Yeah, get over yourself! Do some real damage," Kathy adds, unnecessarily.

"Not all of us can be personality hires," Janice returns in a scoff, but there's no real malice in it. I'm not sure if she means it as a compliment or not. Kathy takes it as one regardless.

"It's just not a side of myself I would ever normally bring to work," Janice huffs, rolling her eyes at Kathy. She hesitantly meets my eyes again. "You haven't seen the elevator footage, have you?"

"I've seen enough of it," I admit after a few moments. I don't feel like that was the right answer when her brows draw closer in a pinch. "But um, you've read the handbook, right? The Company will respect the rights of all employed monsters' physiological strangeness—"

"I know, I know. It's just. It's weird. You don't really want all your coworkers to have seen your tits. I mean, I dunno, maybe Kathy does."

"I'm not a mammal," Kathy interjects, but Lily, ever a sweetheart, distracts her from elaborating about her avian physiology by picking up some pamphlets on the way into the building.

"I mean. It doesn't have to be weird. I don't have to be weird about it. You can if you want though," I say and realize I'm rambling in an attempt to outmaneuver my own awkwardness.

Janice, however, nods fervently, "I'm not gonna be weird about it if you aren't."

Some small weight lifts off my chest at that, and some part of me loosens my grip on the words that Deanna sliced me open with a week ago, and how the Cult of Productivity lady made me feel. I'm not about to forget them, but maybe things aren't as dire as I'd been anticipating.

At least, maybe they won't be if I have a few friends at work.

I hate that I took all those awful feelings out on Vlad and pushed him away when all he wanted was the best for me. The thought of what I'm going to say to Vlad when I see him, if I see him, is starting to dawn on me. I don't have a plan. Maybe I should have prepared notecards. No, that would just make it clear I don't know what to say.

The tradeshow is as expected: loud and easy to get lost in. There are escalators leading every which way, and yet none of them seem to be going where I need them to. It's being hosted in the Endless Symposium Hall, and so the tradeshow map unfolds infinitely. Folding it all back together is a hassle, and what starts as a little trifold pamphlet is now a jumble of paper that is too thick to fit back in my dress's pockets.

And if I'm going to have to look people in the eyes and shake their hand, it's nice that they hand me a little keychain or stress ball every time. I have ten clicky-pens, two multi-color pens, a laser pointer, and a stress ball shaped like a mini barcode scanner. It is extremely satisfying.

One of the booths has a gimmick where they take your business card in exchange for a tiny latte made fresh there. The quality of coffee is good enough that I go back twice. I can't say I'm not having just a little bit of fun.

Eventually, I see our company, and I want to run. Distantly, I hear Lily laugh, and Janice talking about something, and I try to find someone's hand to grab for moral support.

I try not to clench my teeth anxiously, because Dr. Lucille just lectured me about my tooth grinding habits, but it's hard not to with every step closer to our company's booth. Before I know it, I'm holding my breath like I'm about to dive underwater.

"No doubt it's revenge for being relocated to the basement. I mean, it's not our fault it was available when that nymph decided to make the most dramatic of resignations and their floor got flooded," Janice is saying, and I start to turn around to look for Kathy. Maybe she'll let me hold her talons for a moment while I steady myself, and—

My next step is like I walked right into a wall.

I stagger back a step, and a hand catches mine, steadying me. I feel my heart drop in my stomach. I know the warm, leathery feeling of these hands.

Vlad.

When I open my eyes and see him, it breaks my heart a little to see how tired he looks. Maybe I'm imagining it, but there are unfamiliar shadows underneath his eyes, the lines of his face are carved deeper than I remember. I'm not imagining the way his hand tightens around mine.

"Oh," comes out of my mouth before I can think to hide my surprise.

Kathy strolls up and chirps unhelpfully, "Oh, hey, boss. I told you I got Gwen to take the extra badge, right?"

"You did not," he says, his eyes becoming a mask of emotion as he looks down upon me. He lets go, and my hand falls back to my side.

Evil Overlord, save me.

I've been just kind of standing here in the small aftermath of our collision, as if it were an earthquake. The breath in my chest is like coming up from underwater, returning to the moment where we are.

Of course, Deanna is there.

"Baby girl, you gotta keep your head on a swivel," she coos. "They really need to implement some traffic rules here."

"Ideally, your friends would have your back," I reply, and leave it at that. I don't care enough about her to want to get her back like Kathy suggested, but one of these days I'll probably make a point of saying someone else is the nicest person in the office and watch her entire identity crumble around a single comment.

Right now, my attention is more focused on Vlad. He fiddles absently with the cuffs of his sleeves, flexing the hand that caught mine as if to shake off the sensation.

Mistake, mistake, mistake, my heart thuds in my chest.

I grind my teeth a little, as a treat. It doesn't help much.

Vlad looks just a touch wary as he glances to me. I don't blame him. I don't know what kind of relationship we have now. Strangers, to awkward acquaintances, to coworkers, to friends with benefits, to nearly romantic. I guess we're back to just being coworkers again.

He raises a granite eyebrow at the hoard I've collected. "Discovering a new taste for handshakes?"

"Um, free pens, mostly."

"Your inbox is going to be destroyed by tomorrow," he murmurs, a morbid fate if his tone is anything to go by.

I chew my tongue on a response that he's allowed to destroy my inbox any time he likes, because I should probably get to my apology before I make remarks like that.

"It's ok, my email address is one letter off on the card. They printed them wrong when I first started working here. I did that on purpose, because I don't actually care about generating leads," I ramble, because although it feels like a confession of one of the many ways I'm not a great team player or whatever, it's not the important confession and therefore easier to admit to.

He gives a little laugh, and the sound of it makes my heart ache. I look away quickly, so that the pain doesn't show too evidently on my face.

We fall quiet for a moment, neither of us brave enough to make eye contact for more than a second, and both of us too unsure of what to say next.

This may be my best chance to apologize, I think. It's not ideal. With so many people around us, it might be a little weird to try to bare my heart to him.

"I wanted to—"

"Confidence is a good look on you," he says at the same time I start to speak.

My eyes go wide, and I immediately drop whatever I was trying to say. "Sorry?"

Vlad shrugs, scratching the back of his neck. "You seem . . . happier."

"Oh," I nod. I was really hoping maybe there would be more to that thought, but he doesn't elaborate. "Um, I'm trying to be."

I don't know if that makes sense, really. Suddenly, I've forgotten how to ramble explanations. Something, something, isolation, anxiety, and self-fulfilling prophecies and all that. I don't know if that's really enough to explain it.

Another beat of silence passes while I'm thinking, searching for the right words.

"What were you going to say before?" Vlad asks, and I lose whatever courage I had managed to gather.

I don't know that I can do this, actually.

"Um, there was a booth I wanted to look for. I heard they were giving away free lattes."

The unsureness of the moment stops me from pushing further. If I press too hard on this fragile aching between us, I might break what we have.

The rest of the day at the tradeshow goes similarly. Every little interaction with Vlad is just a little awkward, but they add up, our cooled off relationship warming up just a degree at a time.

It's something, but it's hard not to feel just a little impatient. We don't have a seemingly never-ending trip ahead of us. Tomorrow is a half day of the trade show before we have to pack up the booth and go home.

Like last time, it's more of an event for our people in Sales and business development, and I quickly find there's not much for me to do besides pretend to be interested in our pop-up banners. Kathy enlists me in setting out more copies of our product catalog, table tents with product information, and a CTA to join our mailing list.

As Janice is locking up the products in the under-counter cabinets, she turns to me and says, "A few of us are going out for karaoke, did you want to come with us?"

I blink at her a couple times. She wasn't at the retreat, I suppose, and wouldn't know I avoided the group outings as much as possible.

But then again, I'm here to be with people. I'd rather have a chance to talk with Vlad there than a night in by myself, and even if he isn't there, I need to be around people instead of curling up and hating how lonely I feel.

"All of us?" I ask and try to not glance too obviously towards Vlad.

"Yeah, everyone. There's not that many of us on this trip."

The karaoke bar is right across the street from our hotel, making it absurdly easy to say yes. I let Lily make a show of trying to physically drag me across the street with her, but I don't put up much resistance.

It's a little nicer than other karaoke places I've been to, with separate rooms for small parties. We pile in the room, and I end up in a seat between Janice and Kathy, a little squished together. The table is wet from just being cleaned, and the ice in our drinks attracts condensation almost immediately.

Deanna immediately monopolizes the microphone for the first few songs, nudging people into duets with her. It's loud and unabashed, spilling out into the hallway because the waiter who delivered our drinks left the heavy, sound-proof door open.

"It's nice that you can only make a fool of yourself in front of the people you know, instead of strangers," Soven jokes as he gets up to close it, but the lighthearted effect is somewhat ruined by the general ominous nature he brings everywhere with him.

"Yeah, it's really important I only embarrass myself in front of all of you," I start to add in response as I pass by him, but the humor leaves my words halfway through. It's not really a joke.

I really only want to be a fool and embarrassing in front of people I know and am fond of. Well, maybe except Deanna, she doesn't really meet the criteria. I mean, most coworkers are often little more than strangers. Do I really care what they think of me that much?

The things that I wince at myself for seem less end-of-the-world when I'm around people I enjoy. And when I really think about it, the people who have repeatedly seen me at my worst or weirdest and stuck with me through those moments are also the people I feel safest around. It's hard not to think about meeting Vlad in the airport, and how much I couldn't wait to be rid of him then.

I glance across the booth to Vlad, looking fully at him instead of the glances I'd been stealing. I see him studying me, his body language attuned towards mine.

Evil Overlord, I have been such a fool.

18

I stare at him far too long; it's definitely weird and someone else has probably noticed by now, but the only thing that breaks my reverie is the music coming to an end.

Before I know it, I'm out of my chair, ducking under the table to scoot out onto the little stage area. I take the microphone and scroll through the karaoke catalog quickly until I find a song I know.

"Um, I don't know if any of you have had the pleasure of listening to a siren sing before, but, uh, I'm afraid I'm going to have to disappoint you."

The raised eyebrows of my coworkers barely register. If they didn't know after Deanna told people, well then, now they do. I thought if I didn't let people know anything about me, I could keep myself safe, but it wasn't true. It just stopped me from making connections with people I could have been really close with.

I don't care that I'm making the most obvious heart eyes at Vlad. I've answered the door in my underwear enough that this should be easy in comparison. Really. Except, I'm only trying to seduce one of them, and they're all about to witness this.

Vlad's eyes are on me, bright and curious. He's leaning in, the same level of heat in his eyes that I feel in my cheeks. I try not to do anything so obvious as twirl my hair and giggle as it strikes me, that even after every awkward moment in the airport and between PowerPoint presentations, he kept talking to me. It's kind of a weird thought, that anyone would look at me like this after seeing me at my crustiest and cringiest.

There's so much warmth and gratitude in my chest, and not just from the alcohol. I haven't had that much yet. But he's been more generous with me than I've been to myself, kinder and more supportive.

The music starts to play. I wince at myself a few times, and then just launch into it as if I were in my car on the freeway driving eighty-five MPH.

Janice has the best poker face of the lot, Kathy has both hands over her mouth, but her eyes are wide, presumably because she didn't know just how bad of a singer I am.

"Is she supposed to be bad?" Kathy fails to whisper quietly. Lily, ever a dear, shushes and elbows Kathy in the side.

It doesn't matter; the look on Vlad's face is enough to keep me going. I have never seen him look so awed, his eyes soft and adoring, even when my voice cracks every few notes.

I can't tear my eyes away from his, and dance to the music just a little, throwing my hand in his direction, winking cheesily, and curling a finger at him.

I stumble over some of the words, a verse I never bothered to learn the lyrics for catches me unawares. I start losing some of my volume, and therefore my momentum. I stammer a second, the music continuing on without me.

Vlad's voice comes in with the ring of another cheap microphone, and I look up. He's picked up the second one that not many people had actually been dueting with.

He's also bad, but he's also not trying to hit the notes and spectacularly missing the way I am.

Kathy tries to boo us off the little stage, Janice helps her. I honestly don't care. If anything, it makes me sing louder and just a little more off key.

The moment moves me in a way that is less dancing and more flailing vaguely to the beat while giggling and staring in his eyes. Every sour note comes with a smile, and it's every feeling I wanted to give him, everything I couldn't put into words.

The song ends, and the world is just this dark corner with only us.

There's some polite, some enthusiastic, applause from the seats.

Oh shit, I forgot about them.

I brace myself for the inevitable cringe, the knee-jerk need to curl in on myself, and it never comes. There's too much else happening, my work friends smiling and Vlad leading us back to the tables, where he sits next to me this time.

The giddiness of the moment lasts in a way that I always hoped it would. Glasses clink against the table, music conducts one wonderful feeling into the next as the next song comes on, everyone is one eyebrow wiggle away from cracking up again. My face is tired from smiling so hard, but I can't stop.

Vlad's hand is still curled around mine between us as Kathy takes the song selection book and starts flipping through it. I take a sip of my drink and nearly spit it out when

I see Lily practically in Soven's lap, the two nose-to-cowl in conversation.

"What am I seeing?" I murmur, knocking shoulders with Janice.

She follows my eye line.

"An age gap for the record books?" she shrugs, "I guess you wouldn't know. They didn't exactly do paperwork about it."

"A power imbalance to write home about," Vlad observes, and gives me a knowing look.

"No, you don't know Lily. She's terrifying when she wants to be," I explain. "She scares me more than he does."

"Yeah, and you saw why Randall didn't get an exit interview," Janice chuckles darkly into her drink.

"They seem suited for one another, in a weird way. They're well matched."

I feel Vlad's hand tighten over mine at my comment, and then release just enough, as if it hadn't happened at all.

I don't know how to begin to ask him if something is wrong, before he lets go of my hand, standing and casually exiting to the hall.

My heart pounds in my chest, counting several moments. Or maybe just a few seconds. Janice calls something teasing to Lily about PDA, and Lily sends a quick gesture back in return.

I feel somewhat removed from it all, and even the music sounds distant.

I swallow and push off the seat again, scooting out the long way around a table to follow after Vlad.

As soon as I step into the hallway, I see the doorway to the rooftop not quite closing behind him. It's at least ten degrees cooler outside on the roof, and jarringly quiet.

The silhouette of Vlad against the night sky is unmistakable, the light from the moon carving out the details that feel so completely him. The wide stance, the close-tucked wings, tail flicking to echo his thoughts. He's chosen a spot on the far side of the roof, one hand above his head against a billboard's scaffolding as he leans against it, swirling a glass of some liquor in the other as he contemplates his view.

He looks back when the door swings shut behind me, and sees me, fully creeping on him. He tips his glass to me, and I tilt my head just enough to acknowledge it.

"Hey."

"Hey yourself."

We haven't been alone together like this since the fight. The privacy feels almost suffocating. The weight of his stare is almost too much to bear. I drop my eyes to the gritty cement of the roof, watching the stillness of his tail.

That sight opens up the dam in me. I start rambling everything I've been holding in all at once.

"I'm sorry I yelled. And, basically, for every part of what happened. I got a little too much in my own head, and I wasn't really mentally available to deal with anything—"

Vlad looks like he wants to cross to me but doesn't let himself. "Gwen, no. You don't have to explain. I'm sorry I made you feel burdened by my expectations."

"No, you gave me a wonderful compliment, and I wish I had been able to really receive it. I shouldn't have lashed out like that," I tell him earnestly. "I don't really let anyone in. I haven't in so, so long. I've forgotten what it means to have a deep connection with someone, that their mere presence in your life can make you want to be better. And you . . ."I trail off. I can feel the weight of the moment, what it means to put myself out there, put my feelings on the table, exposed and vulnerable. He could reject them as easily as I had rejected his, and he would have every right to. I swallow, feeling myself lock up and start to hedge.

"I'm just glad to know everything is ok between us," I tell him.

It feels a little like a lie. I'm honestly very stressed that it might stay like that. Merely being ok might be as cruel a fate as thinking he hates me.

I would have said yes, I want to tell him. I need to. Maybe that's too much to pack into this moment, but I know I have to tell him.

"When you asked if I'd ever come back to your lair," I start to press lightly on the sensitive subject. There isn't a good way to ask someone to open their heart back up to you after you've rejected them. "I wish I'd been in the right mind to give you a thoughtful answer. But if . . ."

He gives his head a little shake, and I press no further.

"You've given me a lot to think about . . . I don't know that I've seen enough of you," he says, a faint smile gracing his face.

The muted pulse of music and laughter from behind the karaoke booth's heavy door is numbing when my body is itching for something more definite.

Normally, I file away this kind of sensation for therapy, but I don't think I can.

Well, I got what I came here for. I apologized. And I think he accepted it. It still feels like a loss. I'm not ready to return to the party, to plaster on a smile I don't mean, but I don't know what else to do right now.

Fuck it, show him your tits.

"You need to see more of me? Watch me," I tell him. Ironically, this is a much more comfortable option than karaoke, I should have just led with this. There are only so many times I can dodge that intrusive thought anyway.

Being weird seems to have been the one thing that's really ended up working for me, anyway. And if there's a better way to express how deeply devoted and loving you feel towards someone than being weird in his general direction, well, then, I wouldn't know about it.

I turn my face away, but my attention remains on him, and what I can show him. My hands trace casually down my body from my collarbone, pulling apart all the tiny buttons that hold the top of my dress together. Biting my lip, I dare a glance, first down to the unaware traffic below us, and then the statue-like figure blending into the architecture of the building's roof line.

If I'm not mistaken, his glass has found the floor, and his hands are curled tight at his sides.

My teeth worry into my lower lip, appreciating the way he stands back and puts his hands into his pocket, emphasizing the broadness of his shoulders.

Even without being able to make out his expression, I can see it for the smolder it is.

The look he gives me from across the way ignites from my chest down past my navel, my knees feeling suddenly unsupportive. I can't make out his amber eyes from this far a distance, but the way he tilts his head appraisingly makes me feel just how empty my cunt is at this moment, and I'm suddenly dripping wet with need.

He starts undoing his tie like he's got a vendetta against it. He throws it aside like it's nothing to him, and if that doesn't make me all the wetter. He undoes his cufflinks one at a time, and I think I may run out of clothes before he does. I may have to resort to fingering myself on this rooftop to put on a real show for him.

I'm fully unbuttoning the blousy front of my dress, shrugging the shoulders off. The wind pulls it away, and it's gone in a shimmer of darkness and clouds.

"I want to give myself to you. My body, my heart, everything in between."

Then it's just me, standing naked in my heels on this rooftop.

I glance to the far end of the rooftop, and it's empty.

Everything in my world stills for a second, wondering if he left, how he could have simply left, before a shadow cuts through the moonlight above me.

I catch sight of him then, wings stretched out and carving deftly through the air before he lands before me and scoops me up. My sense of balance is tumbling like laundry in the wash, but I don't care. He's holding me.

My arms are around his neck, touching his horns, his face, his chest, unbuttoning the rest of his shirt. He shrugs out of it easily, and I stifle a laugh that it's still tucked in and hangs over his belt.

"You're still Mr. Overdressed," I tease.

"That's it. No more Mr. Nice Guy," comes a growl from deep in his throat, or maybe it's from his mouth and I'm just intently watching the way he undoes his belt in a single deft motion. My heart is between my legs, my wrists are pinned above my head in his hands. I let out a gasp as his belt slips through and tightens around my wrists. My pulse quickens at the thought of what he might be intending this for.

Then he lifts me off the ground by my bindings. One of my shoes comes off, and I have to press my knees hard together at the way my body sings with need.

My arms pull together over my head, and my back arches into the movement, pushing my breasts out, impatient to have more of his touch.

And, fuck, I'm so wet, I'm ready for anything right now.

"It's time for Mr. Extra Nice Guy," he says.

I lift my head, frowning. I go to lean forward a bit to maybe ask him what that's about, but my elbows don't have the leverage for that.

Vlad takes my current immobility to trace a claw against my cheek, down my collar bone to my navel.

"You have lovely ideas, and it's clear you aren't appreciated as you need to be. But you pretend you don't want to be appreciated. You go as far as to remove yourself from opportunities to be appreciated," he continues.

I yank on the knot around my wrists, but it's a good knot, and snug to boot. I yank away with every muscle in my body, and the motion sends me swinging away from him.

He wraps a massive hand around my back, pulling my body closer to him as he leans over me.

"Do you think if you make it harder for people to love you, and they're still there, that will prove to you finally that you're worthy of being loved?"

The urge to deflect is hard to wrangle, and it nearly beats me. I blow the hair out of my face. I'm sure my expression is anything except appreciative right now.

"I'm trying to learn how to take you at your word, the first time," I admit. "It's hard. I'm sure it'll take a bit of practice."

He presses a kiss to my forehead and plants a little plasticky star sticker on my cheek.

"Y'know, I've changed my mind. Maybe they are a little patronizing."

"Maybe you can start with learning to take praise unchallenged."

I'm going to break up with my telehealth therapist. Why am I going to therapy when I can have a gargoyle pin me down and make me unpack my baggage?

"Ok, I'll work on accepting compliments, you don't have to tie me up to get that to happen," I tell him, when he gives a little tug at the belt I'm suspended from. The motion is dizzying and oddly arousing. Just when I think my cunt can't feel any needier . . .

Vlad drags his tongue across my breast, gathering the nipple into his mouth to suck, and consequently drive me crazy.

To be touched by him only emboldened me further.

I don't quite have the core strength to lift my legs up over his shoulders like this, but he does most of the work himself, spreading my legs with his free hand, and then lowering me bodily to fit my cunt against his mouth like a delicacy he can't wait to taste.

His mouth is hot and everything I need, capturing the pulse still thrumming between my legs with his tongue. I whine desperately for more, and he obliges, burying his mouth between my thighs, his tongue scalding as it alternates between long licks through my folds, and delving deeper and deeper inside me. All of it layers pleasure and heat exquisitely against the tension in my shoulders and arms.

I keen loudly as my climax nearly breaks me, and then he's lowering my body down, to rest against his chest. The binding loosens around my wrists, and I almost didn't realize how much I needed that, red lines already creased into my skin.

As much as I want to look up and trace the lines in his face lovingly, my arms are too exhausted to do anything but drape over his shoulders.

"It's nice that we're cool now," I murmur against his warm stoney chest. "Otherwise, this would be a bit awkward."

His laugh is so low, I barely hear it over the wind up on the rooftop, but I feel it through his ribcage against mine.

We linger there a few moments, watching the wisps of clouds drift by. The view over the city, stars above and below, reminds me of the last time we stood outside, and he talked about the ways we could build a life together. I find myself bringing it up without thinking.

"Vlad, if we're going to do this, we need to have a conversation about how we're going to work together. I mean like actually work. Because if you want to keep trying to help me be some kind of high-powered career woman . . ." I trail off, because I can't even fathom trying to be like that. It makes me too tired to even try to form a sentence about it. I shake my head. "That's not me."

He pulls back enough to hold me in his eyes, touching the side of my face with such a tenderness, I know I trust him before he even says anything.

"Gwen. I don't need you to be that. I just want to see you do the things that you're passionate about, and support you how you need me to," he says, before he grimaces at himself. "As far as pitches go, I think my last one went pretty badly."

"I don't think we can blame you for bad timing. Or my industrial grade shell. But if your offer's still on the table . . ."

"We can circle back if you're still interested," he chuckles, stroking his smooth granite palms against my back contemplatively. He pauses, and just as I'm wondering where his mind has gone, he says, "I suppose people will ask if I've been seduced by the siren."

I cringe at myself, even through my grin. There we go, the consequences of my actions. I'm not dreading them as much as I thought I might. "There were some witnesses. I don't suppose we'll be able to keep it to ourselves."

"I'll have to tell them she sang to me, and it was enchanting."

"Well, it is traditional," I blush. I hold myself back from apologizing for it. I can't when he so clearly enjoyed it.

"Then I owe you a mating in the way of the gargoyle," he murmurs.

I bite against my smile, but it's too wide to contain. "I'll take you up on that. Um. Sometime. Whenever is good for you."

He lays his shirt over a squarish vent hood on the roof and sets me down there.

I don't know what it says about me that stripping down to nothing up here is fine, being eaten out on the rooftop is fine, but him putting his crisp, over-ironed shirts on the gritty cement up here like it's nothing makes me wonder if we should take this indoors. Not that we wouldn't just break his bed again. I hope he has a more durably constructed bed back in his lair.

I almost protest, but bite my mouth closed on it. It's a sweet gesture, and it makes me feel treasured. There is only a slight precipice of unsureness left in the back of my mind, that even after all this, we haven't committed where we are with each other to speech yet.

In my silence, he crouches before me, and the tensile strength of his slacks only barely contains his hardened cock. We're not quite done up here. I watch the little smile tug at his mouth as he traces gentle caresses over my wrists, smoothing out the lines he pressed into them.

"If it convinced you of my intentions, I would mate you tonight."

"Mate," I repeat. That was a little more serious than "girlfriend" which I'd figured might take a little time to work up to. Might be moving a bit fast. It's a little more forward than the human men I've dated, but then again, I wasn't human, was I? I could follow my own schedule.

A moment has passed without my answer, I realize when I catch his eyes again.

"You mean out here?" I can't help but ask, glancing at our surroundings. It may be warm this evening, the night dark and cloudy, but from this rooftop I can still see into people's apartments, and occasionally make out people.

My response makes him grin.

"You think anyone will see us through their little windows?" He asks with an amused smile. I was just looking in, no reason someone might not look out.

I shake my head. I don't think anything can possibly ruin this moment. "I think we're high up enough."

"Not quite . . ."

Vlad unsheathes his cock from his pants, discarding them to the roof beside me. My mouth waters a little at the way it juts forth, thick and ready. That would have to wait for another time, it seemed, as he held out a hand to me.

I put my hand in his, standing for barely more than a second as he scooped me up again. I was ready for it this time and wrapped my legs around his waist.

He readies the tip of his cock at my entrance, then meets my eyes. I give a little nod, my arms around his neck once again.

Whatever I thought last time was like does not set enough of a precedent for what mating a gargoyle is like. He beats his wings, mere physics driving his cock inside me. The force of it is so sudden, leaving my body ringing with its impact, I barely noticed at first that he's taking us into the sky.

Each beat of his wings has him delving deep into me, hard and fast. Each time I think I lose all the breath in my body. It's like being held and rocked by the ocean, the deep night sky swallowing us, wave after wave, climbing ever higher.

With each flap of his wings, the world—the sky moves around us, thrusting his cock hard into me, withdrawing for a brief moment that makes my heart stop each time it happens, that gravity begins to catch up with us for a life-rending second, before he beats his wings again, pumping his hips into mine in a force that makes me see different stars.

I unravel well before him, but the endless bone shattering thrusts draw my climax out and coax forth another one, all of it melding together. Vlad lets out a deep growl as he claims me, and moments later, I feel his hot sticky satisfaction dripping down my thighs.

Finally, he lets the wind fill his wings, fanning out wide. Wisps of clouds drift by like seafoam on the beach. It's so quiet up here, with just the two of us, cradled by the night.

I look down at the flecks of lights littered below us in the endless dark city, then back to Vlad, his adoring gaze from between my arms clutched around his neck. An unfamiliar feeling slips in through all my sundered defenses—being watched over.

I close my eyes and bask in it.

19

Volunteering information had never been my strong suit. I take a deep breath and remind myself I'm capable of something as small as this. I have quashed beef between minotaurs, mediated for gaslit cyclops, and done couples counseling between hydra heads.

I can talk to my boyfriend.

Boyfriend. It does make me smile and roll over girlishly, kicking the sheets of his big, sturdy bed. *Our* big sturdy bed. I do live here now. We did go find a bed we liked and was comfortable enough for the both of us, because it turned out that the bed Vlad had before me was only so durable. It didn't give up the ghost as quickly as the hotel bed did, but it also didn't last our entire first month living together.

I keep trying to fall back asleep, but my nerves are gnawing me awake every time I turn my pillow over. I'm going to tell him.

I hear the sound of a cup being set down on the nightstand near me, and when I roll over, the morning light is filtering through the steam coming off my coffee, and the gargoyle who made it for me.

I don't know if that's ever going to get old.

I push up to a sitting position, stretching and moving closer to him. I kneel on the edge of the bed and start undoing the buttons of his shirt even as he's fixing his cuffs. This is the game we end up playing most mornings, figuring out if I can convince him to be a little bit late.

"Are you going to get dressed?" he asks, eyeing the fact that I'm still curled up in the bedsheets. "Or is it a work from home day for you?"

My hands stammer over a button, and his catch up to mine in that split second, rebuttoning deftly. He places a kiss on the top of my head.

"Neither, actually."

"You're taking the day off?" he asks before he checks his watch and mutters a curse under his breath. He stands and gives me an apologetic look as he ducks out of the bedroom.

I sigh and think about it to myself. Maybe it can wait.

I watch as he moves to the living room to glance at the news, muted as it flickers across the TV, but the questions run through my mind again and again. I find myself leaning in the doorway, watching him finish getting ready to leave. I chew my lip. Is it too early in the morning for this? Maybe I should wait for later. It's late enough that there's not really time for more than a kiss goodbye.

Vlad checks that he has everything he needs, watch, wallet, keys, before he looks to me again. "You said yesterday you were going to get lunch with Jessica All-Knowing-All-Judging?"

It throws me for a moment, the last thing on my mind. I've been trying to get out more often.

"Um, that's tomorrow. I'm just gonna chill out here today," I shrug, gripping the mug of coffee a little too hard for how hot it is.

Fucking get a grip, Gwen, I tell myself, biting down hard on my lip. *It's not that hard.*

Despite being just about to leave, all his attention focuses on me for a moment. He raises his granite brows, pausing. "What's on your mind?"

He would be able to tell. He's starting to develop an uncanny sense for when I've turned a thought over too many times in my head and need to air it. Sometimes it's nice and it helps me communicate more than I normally would. But I also didn't know it was possible for someone to know you a little too well.

"Two things," I hedge, figuring it might be easier to segue into if I pair it with something, anything. "So . . . I talked to Soven, and I switched to part-time instead of full-time. I'm going to work three days a week, one in the office, the rest from home."

His brows raise even higher, but an interested smile crosses his face and makes my nerves abate a little.

"Part-time," he repeats, sounding interested in where this is going. I appreciate that he's giving me room to explain my trajectory before trying to build a plan around it.

"Yeah, I mean, I know Bill switched to part-time a while back, and he only works half days now. So, the other days I can do what I want. Whatever I want. Art or . . . video games."

I can see the way he starts to say something, before abandoning it. Instead, he comes back to my side, plucking the coffee out of my hand and drawing me in close. He lifts me just enough to bring my face level with his, letting me perch on his arm, his fingers cupping my ass. I've made about a dozen pigeon jokes about this to him, but he's yet to think any of them are funny. Which is fine, they're more for me than anything.

"It's a lot more time than I used to have. I don't want to promise yet that I'm going to finish my degree or start selling my art, because I don't know that's what I want, yet," I tell him, while brushing my nose against his granite cheek.

We're both having a hard time shaking the cult of productivity. Literally. We're both getting emails from that lady to sign up for her e-seminar. I think he struggles a little more with the habits of it, and not making the most out of all his time.

"I'm glad you're making room in your life for your art. And I'm excited to see where that takes you," he says, kissing me sweetly. He stops only to add, "No comment about the video games."

I roll my eyes. He's been coming around on that.

Vlad simply does not understand video games. He's a good sport about cuddling with me while I play them, but he never wants to participate. I guess the man is just a watcher, in more ways than one.

I'm not passionate about working a nine to five, I'm passionate about lounging around in my pajamas. I'm taking being a "self-starter" off my resume and replacing it with "slow-life-enjoyer."

He kisses my cheek again, "You look really happy. I'm really proud of you for being the change you want in your life."

I sigh into the next kiss, "I love you."

It just kind of falls out of my mouth as I'm thinking it. I've thought it a number of times in moments like these, the notion creeping in and making itself at home. I don't think I ever actually intended to say it, at least not yet. I did a lot of math about this; it was definitely supposed to wait another two months.

Vlad just blinks in surprise a moment, and as the second draws out, I worry my teeth into my lip. I don't think I've ever thought he was going to drop me. His eyes soften as he holds my gaze. "Is that the second thing?"

"Oh, no. The second thing is that yesterday I broke a plate," I say in a rush, but the sentence gets lost in another kiss, and by the time it breaks he's laying me down on the mattress again, shrugging out of his shirt.

I guess he *is* going to be late again today.

A Ghost

"We're sorry, your summoning could not be completed. Your ritual is important to us, so please stay on the line."

I groan, pushing back from the chalk diagrams I've drawn on the storage room floor. I clean off my hands as I stand and cross my arms, glaring at the summoning circle.

My emails have gone unnoticed, my calls ring endlessly into the void, and not even an answering machine will allow me to say my piece.

Being undead, I'm functionally immortal. It's not exactly a diagnosis you want to hear.

A lot of people treat the undead as an afterthought. There's a lot of tax information that changes, a lot of bureaucratic red tape on where you land when you go, if you're actually lucky enough to just make it to "dead."

There're many different classifications of undead. There's undying, there's rebirthed, there's reanimated, there's resurrected, to touch on the most common. There's a lot of nuance, and not everyone bothers to learn about it.

I got into a lot of medical debt before I died, and a vampire bought my debt. And until I pay it off, I live in "Suspended Death." Except, since receiving my severance package—being peeled out of my mortal coil, my tangible, physical being—I no longer have an address and have not been receiving my paycheck.

"Your ritual is important to us, so please stay on the li—"

The chalk on the cold cement floor glows an eerie, almost greenish, light, steam wafting up from the portal.

It flickers, and a sound vaguely reminiscent of the dial-up noise thrums through the room. The floor within the circle becomes liquid, transforming into a pit of tar. Shapes push at the boundary between planes, becoming almost human, rasping for air against the pitch and collapsing back into volatile waves.

Maybe it's a little gauche to rip open the fabric of time and space to find someone, the same way that triple texting someone who hasn't replied in a while is a little desperate, but I've run out of fucks to give, as the kids say.

Several minutes pass, watching the tormented souls writhe at the veil between worlds like a bunch of raccoons stuck in a trash bag, making the most horrific smacking and gasping noises known to ASMR.

I check my watch. The hour where the veil is thinnest is almost up. I've been reaching into the void between planes and coming up empty handed.

Whoever is in charge of my paycheck isn't on any unearthly plane either, it seems.

I sigh, uncross my arms, and swipe the tip of my ephemeral shoe through the chalk boundary, erasing the thin bonds of magic.

The chant is swallowed up with the rest of the magic, the waves of shapes falling back into still, cement flooring, dissipating like smoke into the air.

I'll try again tomorrow, I guess. Until then, I can always check my email for new leads.

I settle back into the corner where the IT staff has dumped my old work computer. It's taken months to be able to summon the ability to push the laptop lid open. It may take more time for me to craft an email than it has battery power left on it, but there's always plenty of new reading material.

The fun thing about being dead is you still get emails. The less fun thing is most of the people sending them haven't realized you're dead yet.

This afternoon's messages start with a flagged as important, "HELLO, CAN YOU SUPPORT ME IN THIS ENDEAVOR . . ." that makes my soul shrivel up a little every time I see it. I scroll through a dozen emails that are mostly one-line replies to each other. The answer I'm looking for is probably buried somewhere between layers upon layers of "I am in need of your support," and "Best wishes!"

To top it off, every email is ended by a parade of automatic signatures containing everyone's job titles, phone numbers and email addresses, company logo, company street address, cubicle number, company social media links, and a link to some calendar software.

Of course, the Inlook email program doesn't have a decent search function. It doesn't have decent anything, but the thing about being technologically inept is that it's crucial for surviving the workplace, and that's why we have it instead of a better system.

Then I get another email.

Hi Randall, I miss you.

More Things By Kate Prior

Love Laugh Lich (Claws & Cubicles 1)
Lily has been the Lich's secretary ever since his evilness took over the company. She loves her job, but she's got some questions about her boss. Like what's under that cloak of ever-billowing.
Her wondering intensifies when one day the Lich needs something from her that isn't just scheduling appointments-- but a shiver. He needs it for a spell, but it feels like it crosses a line from their usual banter.
After her contributions to his dark rituals become more than OSHA compliant, sex-magic-and-triple-cocks-oh-my, she starts to contemplate whether the Lich Lord returns her feelings, or still only sees her as his secretary.
Lily may have given him her body, but he never asked for her heart.

The Orc from the Office (Claws & Cubicles 2)
Mate-bonding with a co-worker is against company policy... accidentally or not. Janice knows better than anyone that entanglements with co-workers are risky business.
But when Janice accidentally breaks a co-workers nose, she finds herself unexpectedly mated to an orc, and under Monster Resources' scrutiny. Khent from the IT Department is quiet and nerdy, despite the tusks. His emails are overly wordy. He won't stop apologizing even though she's the one who broke his glasses. Clearly, fate got this one wrong.
All Janice has to do is stay away from Khent until the bond dissipates. Easy enough, right? Except...
…Her company laptop chooses this week to need the orc from the IT Department, repeatedly.
…She accidentally clicks on orc porn at work and has to take remedial phishing training with Khent.
…Their bond will keep pulling them back together until it is completed.

Meet Me at the Anvil
When Diane faints during her wedding vows, it's expected.
Her family thinks almost everything is too stimulating for her
because of her fainting condition. Of course they matched her
with a man who couldn't make anyone's heart flutter.
When her fiancé tries to make light of the situation by giving
her a fainting goat, the ridicule is too much to bear.
Diane wants more than the life before her— she wants to live
the passion and adventure she's only ever found in the erotic
sketches she creates, and the kind of heart-racing feelings her
fiancé's cousin and best man Liam gives her.
The last thing Diane expects as she flees from the church,
however, is for the best man to run away with her.

And They Were Broommates
(A short story included in Hexes and Ohs: A Witch
Paranormal Romance Collection for Charity)
Astrid is breaking her lease. The tower isn't big enough for her
and Jason, and the town only needs one resident witch. She's
tired of competing with him over every little thing.
Except, the lease-breaking ritual goes wrong, and they end up
with a strange bond letting them hear everything the other is
thinking. They didn't need a psychic link to know they hated
each other, but now they can't hide everything else they think
about each other.

If you enjoy learning about the craft of writing or finding solidarity in the ups and downs of publishing, listen to the podcast *Romance Writer's Therapy*, hosted by Kate Prior and Marty Vee.

You can follow Kate on socials: Instagram, Twitter, Threads, or Tiktok @bykateprior, or join her reader's group on Facebook, *Kate's Priory of Paranormal Romance*.

Find book updates, content warnings, and subscribe to her sporadic newsletter at kate-prior.com.

www.ingramcontent.com/pod-product-compliance
Lightning Source LLC
Chambersburg PA
CBHW070509160726
48003CB00004B/1487